TOURNAMENT OF TERROR

by Neo Edmund

Penguin Young Readers Licenses
An Imprint of Penguin Random House

D0447220

PENGUIN YOUNG READERS LICENSES
An Imprint of Penguin Random House LLC

Cover illustration by Dan Panosian

ISBN 9780515159714   10 9 8 7 6 5 4 3 2 1

Chapter 1

In the Command Center of the Mighty Morphin Power Rangers, Kimberly Hart watched nervously as the seconds ticked away on a clock above one of the many blinking computer consoles. In only five minutes, a space bridge would teleport the Rangers to a strange world on the far end of the galaxy. The details of their dangerous mission were an absolute secret. If the evil witch Rita Repulsa were to learn of their plans, she would do everything in her power to stop them.

Alpha 5, the Command Center's robotic caretaker, scurried around in a panic. "Aye-yi-yi! We're running out of time, and we still don't have the final coordinates to align the space bridge," he said.

"Relax, Alpha." Billy Cranston, the Blue Power Ranger, was typing complex calculations on a computer tablet. "I'll have the coordinates ready in time," he said.

"It's not that we don't trust you," said Jason Scott, the Red Ranger. He was doing a final check on the special weapons they were taking on the mission. "We just don't want to miss dinner."

Billy grimaced. "When did that ever happen, except for that one time?" he asked.

Zack Taylor, the Black Ranger, carefully packed survival meal kits into a backpack. "Twelve ration packs should be enough to feed four Rangers for three days, right?" he asked.

Trini Kwan, the Yellow Ranger, finished rolling up a survival tent. "News flash—there are five Rangers, not four."

Zack looked curiously at Kimberly. "Haven't you told them yet?" he asked.

"Told us what?" Jason asked. He and the others approached Kimberly.

Kimberly was surprised her friends hadn't realized what was going on. Unlike them, she wasn't wearing her Ranger suit. "You guys know being the Pink Ranger is the most important thing in the world to me," she said.

"Kimberly, what's going on? Are you sick?" Billy said.

Their leader, Zordon, an ancient galactic sage trapped in a time warp, looked down on the Rangers from inside an energy chamber that served as his link to the Command Center. "Fear not, Rangers. Kimberly isn't sick. She has, however, decided to stay behind for a personal reason," he said.

Kimberly frowned. She was feeling a little guilty. "The Angel Grove Gymnastics Tournament is this weekend. If I go on the mission, I'd miss my chance to compete," she said.

"Kimberly, you have to go for it," Trini said. "If you win, you could go on to the Pan Global Games. That's been your dream since you were a little girl."

"This is far too important an opportunity to pass up," Billy said.

"I know, but it also feels wrong to ignore my duty as the Pink Ranger over a silly tournament," Kimberly said.

Zordon proudly smiled. "Kimberly, your loyalty to the Power Rangers is admirable, but there is nothing silly about pursuing your dreams," he said.

Jason nodded in agreement. "Then it's settled. We handle the mission. You stay here and win that tournament," he said.

Kimberly smiled warmly. "You guys are the best friends ever."

She watched timidly as Jason, Zack, Billy, and Trini gathered their equipment and then stepped up onto a metal platform. The clock over the main console counted down from thirty seconds.

"Rangers, the space bridge won't open again for seventy-two hours," Zordon said. "Whatever happens on your mission, you are all on your own. Look out for one another and may the Power protect you."

"You have our word, Zordon," Jason vowed.

Kimberly felt shaken by Zordon's warning, because it also meant she would be on her own if trouble were to arise in Angel Grove.

"Beginning final countdown," said Alpha 5. "Ten, nine, eight . . ."

"Entering coordinates now," Billy said. His fingers moved at lightning speed as he typed on the tablet. A glowing energy ring began to spin around the platform.

"Opening space bridge in three, two, one," Kimberly said. She pushed a button on the main console marked ENGAGE.

An energy vortex appeared above the platform.

The Rangers morphed into four beams of energy—red, blue, yellow, and black. They then vanished into the vortex.

Kimberly looked to the clock. The time was now counting down: 71 HOURS, 59 MINUTES, 55 SECONDS.

Alpha 5 put a hand on Kimberly's shoulder to comfort her. "Don't worry. The Rangers will be just fine," he said.

Kimberly half-heartedly nodded in agreement. "I know they will. I just hope I'll be okay without them."

Chapter 2

Meanwhile, the evil space sorceress bent on world domination, Rita Repulsa, stood on an observation deck atop the tallest tower of her lunar fortress known as the Moon Palace. While spying on the people of Earth through her long-range telescope, she saw four beams of light soaring away from the planet.

She turned a crank on the telescope to zoom in for a closer look.

"Well, well, my nemesis Zordon is using a space bridge to send those meddlesome Power Rangers on some sort of mission," Rita said. She turned to face her grisly gang of alien sidekicks. "Why didn't anyone tell me about this?" she asked.

"A thousand apologies, my queen," said Finster, an intellectual gray-skinned alien with pointy ears and a long snout. "We do our best to track Zordon's activities, but he's always one step ahead of us."

Rita grinned with wicked delight. "No matter.

With the Rangers away, it's time for me to play," she said.

Baboo, a lanky apelike alien with blue skin and black fur, looked at the four beams of light that were heading off into space. "Red, blue, yellow, and black. Pardon me, my queen, but aren't there five Rangers?" he asked.

Rita picked up a long staff that had a golden crescent moon mounted on the top. She used it to smack Baboo on the head.

"Of course there are five Rangers, you dim-witted fool," she said.

Squatt, a short and pudgy alien with a big head and huge teeth, lumbered up to Rita. "But if only four Rangers are going on the mission, someone must have stayed behind," he said.

"Silence, you fool," Rita said, and shoved Squatt out of her way. She again looked through the telescope and saw the four beams of light. "Red, blue, yellow, and black. That means that infuriating Pink Ranger is home all alone."

Finster grinned proudly. "This is just too good. We could destroy Zordon and stop the Rangers from returning to Earth," he said.

"What are you babbling about?" Rita asked curiously.

Finster hurried over to a large object concealed beneath a greasy tarp. "I'm talking about my electromagnetic pulse bomb, or EMP for short," he said, and pulled away the tarp, revealing a metallic sphere covered with tubes, frayed wires, and flickering lights. "In one fell swoop, we could permanently disable the Command Center and take out every electrical device in Angel Grove."

Rita kicked the EMP. "I thought you said this hunk of tin was a big fat dud," she said.

"My invention is no dud, your evilness," Finster said. He pointed to a power gauge on the side of the EMP. The needle was at the empty line. "I said we need a massive source of energy to charge it to full capacity."

"What about the Angel Grove Power Station?" Baboo asked.

Finster considered this. "Yes, I believe the power station would do the trick, but the EMP would take nearly three days to charge. We'd have to find a way to keep that pesky Pink Ranger from discovering it," he said.

Rita pondered wicked thoughts.

"So, how to stop the Pink Ranger from interfering." Her eyes narrowed with a dastardly idea. "I've got it. Somebody tell that no-good Goldar to get his metal tail in here," she said.

Goldar, a monstrous, apelike alien warrior with jet-black wings and golden armor, stepped up behind Rita. "You called, my queen?" he asked.

Startled, Rita turned around. "How did you get here so quickly?" she asked.

Goldar shrugged. "I've been here the entire time," he said.

Rita smacked him with her staff. "Just shut your trap and follow me."

Rita led Goldar down a long and dreary stone corridor.

They passed several metal cell doors, each with a vicious creature growling on the other side. They then walked through a crackling energy barrier and entered an octagon-shaped chamber. In the center was a black pedestal with a glowing pink chest sitting atop.

Rita opened the chest, revealing an ancient amulet hanging from a golden chain. Goldar leaned in for a closer look. He saw a tiny gem in the middle of the amulet that was glowing bright with pink energy.

"I've been saving this for the perfect opportunity," Rita said. "With this mystical amulet, you will be invisible to all humans except for the Pink Ranger."

"And how will this help me destroy her?" Goldar asked.

Rita put the amulet around Goldar's thick neck. "You're not going to destroy her. Your job will be to terrorize her night and day. Whenever she turns around, you'll be there, but with nobody else able to see you, she'll think she's going off like a cuckoo clock. Her mind will become so tired and confused that she'll do anything to get you to leave her alone. That's when you will order her to take you to the Command Center," she said.

"Now I understand," Goldar said with a raised fist. "With the Pink Ranger's help, I could get into the Command Center undetected. I would knock Zordon out of commission before he even knew I was there. There would be nobody to stop us from detonating Finster's EMP."

"And when the Command Center is permanently disabled, the Rangers won't be able to return to Earth,"

Rita said with vile delight. "It's a perfect plan, so you better not screw it up."

"As you command, my queen," Goldar said. Then he teleported away in a streak of gold light.

Chapter 3

At the Angel Grove Youth Center, the gymnastics tournament was in full swing. A young gymnast was performing a dazzling tumbling routine to the delight of the cheering crowd.

While Kimberly watched from the sideline before her turn to perform, she began to feel nervous about her chances of winning. This was the first time she had ever competed against gymnasts with such high-level skills.

A teen girl named Sarah Robins stepped up next to Kimberly. She was wearing a T-shirt that said TEAM KIMBERLY in bright pink letters. On the back was a logo for the Angel Grove Center for the Hearing Impaired.

The crowd burst out cheering as the other gymnast finished her performance. "She's really good," Kimberly said to Sarah.

Sarah grinned at Kimberly and then pointed to her own ears.

Kimberly grimaced, having nearly forgotten that Sarah was deaf. She started using her hands to speak in sign language. "I said she's really good," she signed.

Sarah signed in response, "You are also really good, so don't worry. I know you will be amazing."

"Thank you. That means a lot to me," Kimberly replied.

On the intercom, an announcer said, "Next up, Angel Grove's own Kimberly Hart!" The crowd burst out in thunderous cheers.

Sarah joined a group of teens in the front row. They were all students at the Angel Grove Center for the Hearing Impaired and wore TEAM KIMBERLY T-shirts.

Together, they signed: "We believe in you, Kimberly!"

Kimberly smiled and waved to her friends. She walked over to the far corner of the tumbling floor. She pictured herself doing the opening steps of her routine. This was hardly necessary because she'd practiced so much she could perform the routine in her sleep.

On the intercom, a catchy rock song Kimberly had chosen for her routine began to play. She took a deep breath and launched into her opening run. With amazing skill, she executed a series of soaring half-twists and backflips. The crowd cheered excitedly.

Just as Kimberly prepared for another tumbling pass, a flickering pink light caught her eye. She glanced to the spectator stands and saw a startlingly familiar golden figure lurking among the crowd. "Goldar!" she yelped.

Goldar pointed his hulking sword at Kimberly. "I'm coming for you, Pink Ranger," he said, and then vanished in a blink.

Kimberly nervously looked around, trying to see where Goldar had gone. There wasn't a sign of him anywhere. She rubbed the sweat from her forehead and hoped that it was just her nerves playing tricks on her.

It took Kimberly a few calming breaths to regain her concentration. This was no time to fall apart, she told herself. A major mistake now would ruin her chances of moving on to the next round of the tournament.

As Kimberly sprinted into her next tumbling pass, Goldar appeared right in her path. "Surprise," he roared, swinging his bulky sword at her. Deathly startled, Kimberly leaped into a sideways twisting flip, just clearing his blade.

As soon as Kimberly's feet touched the floor, Goldar again swung his sword at her. She backflipped high into the air to dodge the attack. Her heart raced as he swung his sword at her again and again. Each time, she executed an acrobatic move, narrowly evading his strikes.

The crowd responded with gleeful cheers.

"Don't stop now. They love you," Goldar teased.

Kimberly felt confused when she noticed the crowd didn't seem at all concerned. Even Sarah and her friends were smiling and cheering.

While Kimberly was distracted, Goldar grabbed her from behind and locked his muscular arms around her. "I have you now," he said.

Kimberly frantically kicked and flailed around, trying to escape his grip. She then firmly planted her feet on the ground and pushed backward with all her might. Goldar toppled down and lost his grip on her.

"You won't escape me that easily," he said.

Kimberly hopped to her feet. She saw the contest judges were whispering to one another, trying to understand what was happening. She was certain this fiasco must have cost her far too many points to advance in the tournament.

"Don't look so sad. You never had a chance anyway," Goldar said.

Kimberly felt both angry and disappointed. More important, she was worried about the safety of the crowd. She reminded herself that even if they didn't have a clue what was happening, it was her duty as the Pink Ranger to protect them from danger.

"It's time for you to leave, Goldar," Kimberly growled.

"I'd like to see you make me," Goldar said.

Kimberly replied by raising her fists and attacking. She unleashed an astonishing melee of jumping and spinning kicks. Goldar counterattacked with his sword, but Kimberly bashed it out of his hand. She followed up with a spinning kick that knocked Goldar to one knee.

With Goldar stunned out of his senses, Kimberly dashed forward, planted a foot on his knee, and leaped into a soaring backflip kick. The metal brute crashed hard into the floor.

"You lose, Goldar," Kimberly said.

"Maybe this round, Pink Ranger, but our fun has

only just begun," Goldar said. He then vanished in a golden flash.

Kimberly took a long breath of relief, then suddenly remembered where she was. She could feel the eyes of the crowd staring at her. *They must think I've completely lost my mind*, she thought.

After a long moment of silence, Sarah stood up and started clapping. Her friends stood up and joined in. Then the entire crowd burst out in a gleeful standing ovation.

Kimberly dared to look over and saw the judges were also standing and applauding. With a confused shrug and a half-hearted smile, she timidly waved to the crowd.

Chapter 4

In the Angel Grove Youth Center Juice Bar, Kimberly sat at a table with Sarah and some of the students from the Center for the Hearing Impaired. They were celebrating Kimberly's success in the tournament.

Kimberly was having a tough time enjoying the moment. Her strange encounter with Goldar had left her feeling worried and confused. How could she have seen him so clearly but nobody else had?

"Congratulations," Sarah signed. "That was a very unusual routine."

Ernie, the jolly owner of the Juice Bar, walked up and put a tray of fruity drinks on the table. "I'll second that. It was really cool how you mixed all of those martial arts moves into your routine. Where did you ever come up with the idea?"

Kimberly shrugged. "It just kinda came to me in the moment."

Ernie noticed Sarah and the other students

were looking at him with blank stares. "Sorry, my mistake." He then started speaking in sign language, but it was clear to all that he was a newbie. "I said I think it is cool how Kimberly used martial arts in her routine."

Sarah and the others looked at one another and giggled.

"Did I do it wrong?" Ernie nervously asked.

Kimberly signed to Ernie, "They know what you meant to say and are grateful you're trying to learn sign language."

Sarah and the students all smiled and nodded in agreement.

Ernie gave a half-hearted wave and walked away, worried he had made a fool of himself.

Kimberly took a sip of her fruity drink. The sweet flavor brought a calming smile to her face. For the next few minutes, she chatted with Sarah and the other students. They had all been taking sign language lessons from Kimberly and were grateful for the time she volunteered at the Center.

Sarah was grateful for Kimberly's help. She and the other kids in the program had only recently lost their hearing and were having a tough time adjusting. "Will you use martial arts in your balance beam routine tomorrow?" she signed to Kimberly.

"I sure hope not," Kimberly replied, quivering at the thought of fighting Goldar while on the balance beam.

Bulk, a pudgy punk, strutted up to the table. "How about you do some of that screwy sign-lingo in your next routine?" He began to make random hand gestures mixed with ridiculous martial arts–style movements.

Skull, a tall and slender punk, stepped up and made similarly annoying hand gestures. "Yeah, you could call it talking-hand fu?"

Sarah began to weep at Bulk and Skull mocking her. She made a frantic dash for the door.

"What's her problem?" Bulk asked.

Kimberly stood up to follow Sarah, but Bulk and Skull got in her way. "You two really are the biggest pair of jerks I've ever laid eyes on," she said. "Now, out of my way."

"Get out of your way or what?" Bulk smugly asked.

"Yeah, or what?" Skull asked.

Kimberly gave them a sneering glare. "Do you really want to find out?"

Bulk and Skull looked at one another and cringed. They were bullies, but they knew better than to mess with Kimberly.

"Okay, okay, just take it easy," said Bulk, nervously backing away.

"Yeah, no need to get so serious," said Skull, backing away with him.

"Yes, Pink Ranger. Don't be so serious," Goldar said from behind.

Kimberly spun around and was terrified to see Goldar standing only a few steps away from her. "This can't be real. I must be having a nightmare," she said.

"Is that any way to greet your new best friend?" Goldar said.

Kimberly raised her fists, ready for a fight. "You're no friend of mine."

"That's where you're wrong. We're going to be seeing a lot of each other from now on," Goldar replied.

"Who the heck is she talking to?" Bulk whispered to Skull.

"I think all that talking-hand stuff got her brain all mixed up," Skull replied.

Confused, Kimberly looked to Bulk and Skull.

"You really don't see anyone?"

Bulk and Skull just shrugged.

Kimberly noticed everyone in the room was staring at her. She could also tell they were confused by her actions. She looked back to Goldar. "Why can't anybody else see you?" she asked.

"I'll make you a deal." Goldar stepped closer to Kimberly and held out a hand to her. "Take me to the Command Center and I'll explain everything."

"I would never in my entire life take you there," Kimberly insisted.

"You say that now, but you'll change your mind soon enough," Goldar replied.

"Don't count on it," Kimberly said. She walloped Goldar with a powerful side kick. As he stumbled backward, Kimberly noticed Ernie walking by, carrying a large tray of fruity drinks. "Ernie, look out," she yelped.

It was too late. Goldar crashed into Ernie, knocking him down onto a table. Ernie's tray of drinks splashed all over a group of people sitting nearby.

Goldar vanished in a blink.

"Oh no," Kimberly whimpered. She dashed over to help Ernie stand up.

"Nothing to worry about. I'm fine," Ernie said as

he stumbled to his feet. He used his shirtsleeve to wipe his face clean. "I'm just a little confused. What happened?"

"I wish I could explain," Kimberly said. She looked around for Goldar, but it seemed he was gone.

Chapter 5

Kimberly hurried out the front door of the Youth Center. She took a quick look around the area to see where Sarah had gone, but there was no sign of her. Suddenly, a glimmering gold light nearby caught her eye. She snapped a look toward the street, worried that Goldar had returned. She then let out a big sigh of relief when she saw it was just a passing car.

While searching for Sarah, Kimberly thought about the oddity of the situation with Goldar. It just didn't make any sense to her. How could she have seen and felt Goldar so clearly, but nobody else had?

Kimberly then heard a faint whimpering that sounded like Sarah crying, but she couldn't figure out where it was coming from. She continued her search of the area, looking behind the bushes along the building and around the cars in the parking lot.

She thought about calling Alpha 5 to help in the search, but then noticed a pair of pink shoes dangling down from a tree. She cautiously walked over and was surprised to see Sarah sitting on a high branch.

It had been a few years since Kimberly had climbed a tree, but she zipped right up and sat down beside Sarah. "Bulk and Skull are big jerks," Kimberly signed.

Sarah wiped the tears from her eyes. She signed, "You're right. I don't care about them. It's just that—" She stopped short.

"What is it then? You can tell me anything," Kimberly signed.

Sarah hesitated for a moment, and then she finally signed, "My father said the Center for the Hearing Impaired has run out of money and will have to close. I am sad I will not see you anymore."

"I didn't know about that," Kimberly signed. She felt sad because she cared so much for the students at the Center. "That doesn't mean we can't still be friends," she signed.

Sarah smiled and hugged Kimberly.

Kimberly noticed a man frantically dashing around the parking lot. She recognized him as Sarah's father, Jack Robins. "I think your dad is worried about you. We should let him know we're here," she signed to Sarah.

Sarah nodded in agreement.

"Hey, Mr. Robins," Kimberly called out as she and Sarah climbed down the tree.

Jack let out a huge sigh of relief and dashed over. "Sarah, I was so worried. I told you to meet me at the entrance," he signed.

"Don't be too mad, Mr. Robins," Kimberly signed. "Sarah was just telling me how she's sad that the Center has to close."

"Oh, I see," Jack replied. He put an arm around Sarah to comfort her. "Sadly, our funding got cut. Don't get me started on why. But don't be too gloomy about it just yet. There may still be a way to save the Center."

Jack gave Kimberly a flyer, which said:

DO YOU GOT WHAT IT TAKES TO BE

THE *TOUGHEST WARRIOR*???

FIND OUT THIS SATURDAY AT ANGEL GROVE PARK.

WIN HUGE CASH PRIZES.

Kimberly recognized *Toughest Warrior* as the title of a popular TV game show where contestants ran extremely perilous obstacle courses.

"I know what you're thinking," Jack signed, and

then rubbed his pudgy belly. "I'm a bit out of shape, and my chances of winning are next to nothing."

Kimberly carefully considered her response, not wanting to sound rude. "Wow, I thought you had to almost be a pro athlete to make it through that course!"

"You don't have to tell me," Jack said. "But if there's a chance to save the Center, I have to take it."

Kimberly thought about this and realized he was right. "Then maybe I should enter, too. That would double our chances of winning," she said.

"More than double," Jack said gleefully. "With your gymnastics skills, you would be sure to go all the way."

Sarah shook her head in disagreement. "Kimberly, you can't do it. The contest is tomorrow, and it's at the same time as the gymnastics tournament. That's too important for you to miss."

Kimberly slumped in disappointment. "But the Center is important to me too," she signed.

"Don't you worry. I've got it covered," Jack said. "Besides, you already volunteer so much of your time to the Center. It's not fair to ask you to give up your dream."

Kimberly shrugged in half-hearted agreement. "If

only there was a way I could do both."

"Unless you have a jet plane, I don't see how that's possible. The events are on opposite ends of Angel Grove," Jack said.

"I guess you're right," Kimberly reluctantly admitted. "I should get going. I'll see you later."

"Would you like a ride?" Jack offered. "We're heading your way."

Kimberly needed time to think things over, so she thanked Jack for the offer, and instead decided to walk home.

Chapter 6

Kimberly walked briskly along a busy boulevard in Downtown Angel Grove. While waiting for a crossing light to turn white, she pulled the flyer for the *Toughest Warrior* contest from her pocket. She looked at the words WIN HUGE CASH PRIZES and couldn't help but feel a little guilty. If there was a chance to save the Center then she should go for it, she thought.

She recalled how Jack said she would need a jet plane to be able to do the contest and the gymnastics tournament on the same day. "I may not have a jet, but I can use my communicator to teleport from one event to the other," she said to herself.

When the light turned white, Kimberly started to cross the street. She was halfway across when she saw Goldar standing on the other side.

"Did you miss me, Pink Ranger?" Goldar asked, pointing his sword at her.

Startled, Kimberly stopped in her tracks, uncertain

what to do. Drivers began to honk their horns. The crossing light had turned red, and she was now blocking traffic.

In a dash, Kimberly hurried back to the corner from where she had started. Once she was safely on the sidewalk, she looked back, but Goldar was gone. As she raced along in the opposite direction, she repeatedly looked over her shoulder to make sure he wasn't following.

She rounded a street corner and was startled to see Goldar standing in the middle of a crowd. People casually walked by him as if he wasn't there. "Can't get away from me that easily," Goldar taunted.

Kimberly dashed away, but only made it half a block before she again saw Goldar. He was stalking toward her through a busy crowd.

"Goldar, how are you doing this?" Kimberly asked.

Goldar laughed and held out his hand. "I already told you—take me to your Command Center, and I'll explain everything."

"Never!" Kimberly shouted. People walking by looked at her oddly. *This is getting out of control,* she thought, wishing she could teleport to the Command Center. But that just wasn't an option with so many people around.

Goldar was now only a few steps away from her. "Last chance to make this easy on yourself," he said.

Kimberly noticed a city bus pulling to a stop on the opposite side of the street. She checked to make sure it was safe to cross and then quickly dashed for the bus. When she got there, the boarding door was already closing. She called out to the driver, begging him to wait.

The elderly driver just caught a glimpse of Kimberly waving for him to stop. He grumbled and then pulled the lever to open the door. "Consider yourself lucky, young lady," he said, and then checked the time on his wristwatch. "I'm already four minutes behind schedule."

"You're a real lifesaver," Kimberly said, and hurried up the steps to board the bus. The driver glared at her in impatience while she reached into her pocket and searched for coins to pay the fare. She then checked in her backpack, but the only coin she could find was her Power Coin. *There's no way I'm using that,* she thought.

"Young lady, I can't let you ride if you don't have the fare," the bus driver insisted.

Kimberly was startled when she looked out the window and saw Goldar stomping toward the bus. She frantically continued to search around in her backpack. Finally, she found a wadded-up five-dollar bill.

"Any chance you have change?" she asked the driver.

He grumbled and shook his head to say no.

Through the side window, Kimberly saw Goldar was only steps away from the open boarding door. With no other choice, she shoved the five-dollar bill into the fare collector.

"Fine, let's just go," Kimberly said.

"Thought you'd never ask," the bus driver said with a sarcastic grunt. He pulled the lever to close the door and stepped on the gas. Goldar roared furiously as the bus pulled away.

Kimberly walked down the aisle and found an empty seat near the back of the crowded bus. She sat down and took a deep breath of relief. She hoped that Goldar couldn't follow her now.

Chapter 7

The bus started heading into a part of town that Kimberly didn't recognize. She felt anxious when the area became so unfamiliar that she couldn't say for sure if they were still in Angel Grove.

"Excuse me. Where does this bus go?" Kimberly called out to the driver.

The bus driver didn't answer. Instead, he made a hard right and drove down a street in a business district.

"Can you at least tell me if this bus will go back toward Angel Grove?" Kimberly asked. Again, she received no response from the driver.

Kimberly decided this had gone on long enough. Her best bet now would be to get off the bus and teleport to the Command Center. As she walked down the aisle toward the driver, she noticed the other passengers were all wearing hoodies and looking away, as if they were trying to conceal their faces.

When Kimberly approached the driver, she felt a nervous flutter in her stomach. He was much larger and far more muscular than she remembered.

"I'd like to get off at the next stop, please," Kimberly said with a gulp.

"If you want off my bus, you're going to have to pay the fare," the bus driver replied in a deep and rumbly tone.

"But I already paid," Kimberly said in protest. "And a lot more than I needed to, remember?"

"I'm not talking about money," the bus driver said with a wicked cackle. "Your toll is to take me to the Command Center." He then looked back, revealing himself. It was Goldar, wearing a bus driver's uniform.

Kimberly screeched with fright and stumbled backward. Six of the other passengers now blocked the aisle. She saw they all had clumpy gray faces. "Putty Patrollers," she groaned. "I really hate these guys."

Goldar hit the brakes, causing the bus to skid to a stop. "Putty Patrollers, seize the Pink Ranger," he ordered.

The Putty Patrollers grabbed Kimberly's arms to restrain her. "Let go of me," she demanded, and struggled to pull away, but their grip was too strong.

Goldar stood up and leaned in close to Kimberly. She recoiled from the foul stink of his breath. "I'm giving you one last chance, Pink Ranger," he bellowed. "Take me to the Command Center, or my Putty Patrollers will tear you to pieces."

"I would never, ever do that, even if my life depended on it," Kimberly replied.

Goldar laughed. "If you haven't noticed, your life *does* depend on it."

Kimberly knew Goldar was deadly serious. Still, there was no way she would willingly betray Zordon. "I guess I have no choice," she said. Then, still being held by the Putty Patrollers, she raised both legs and double-kicked Goldar in the chest, knocking him backward. His arm smacked into the boarding door control lever as he tumbled to the floor.

The door swung open.

Kimberly flipped backward and rolled over the heads of the Putty Patrollers. When her feet hit the floor, she kicked the nearest Putty in the back, knocking him forward. Two Putty Patrollers turned to attack, but Kimberly punched them both, causing them to flicker and then vanish.

She shoved past the remaining four Putty Patrollers and dashed for the door. Goldar was just ambling to his feet, so Kimberly kicked him again, knocking him into the driver's seat. Then she raced out the door and into the street.

"You'll never escape me, Pink Ranger," Goldar yelled. "You'll see me again soon."

Kimberly knew Goldar was telling the truth. She also knew it was time to figure out what was going on. To do that, she would need the help of Zordon and Alpha 5. She looked around to make sure nobody was watching and then pressed a button on her communicator watch.

In a glimmering flash of pink light, she teleported away.

Chapter 8

At the Command Center, Kimberly sat on a metal stool, fretfully staring at the clock over the control console. There were still sixty hours remaining until the other Rangers were due to return from their secret mission.

Alpha 5 spoke to Kimberly using sign language. "Don't you worry. We'll figure out what that fiend Goldar is up to."

Kimberly smiled. "I see you've been practicing your sign language," she signed.

"And I'm getting better by the day, all thanks to you," Alpha 5 replied.

"That's great. Now can we get this test over with? I'm really anxious to find out what's going on," she said.

Alpha 5 flicked a series of switches on the console. Kimberly held her breath as a wave of light started swirling around her. The light was soon spinning so dizzyingly fast that she had to close her eyes.

A screen on a computer console displayed a digitized outline of Kimberly. Light particles passed through her, scanning for anything unusual. After a moment, the screen flashed green, showing everything was normal.

"Good news, Kimberly. According to the computer, you are in picture-perfect health," Alpha 5 said. He flipped the switches to turn off the scanner.

"That is good news," Kimberly said. "But it still doesn't explain why I keep seeing Goldar, but nobody else can."

"Are you absolutely certain that what you saw was real?" Zordon asked.

"Yes, I'm certain. I'm not going crazy," Kimberly insisted.

"We believe you," Alpha 5 said. He rubbed Kimberly's shoulder to comfort her. "We just need to run more tests. We'll find out what that dastardly Goldar is up to if it's the last thing we do."

Kimberly smiled thankfully, though it didn't make her feel any better.

A red light began flashing and a warning alarm sounded. "Aye-yi-yi! What now?" Alpha 5 cried. On the viewing globe, he saw a dozen Putty Patrollers swarming around a group of industrial workers outside the Angel Grove Power Station. "What could the Putties be up to this time?"

Kimberly looked at the viewing globe and saw Goldar walking toward the station's main entrance. "It's not what the Putties are up to, it's whatever Goldar is up to."

Alpha 5 looked oddly at Kimberly. "Goldar? What do you mean?"

Kimberly pointed at Goldar on the viewing globe. "He's right there. Please tell me you can see him."

Alpha 5 leaned in for a closer look, but he couldn't see Goldar. "I'm sorry, Kimberly. I wish I could say I do but I don't."

Kimberly looked desperately up to Zordon. "Please tell me you can see him," she said.

"While I do sense the presence of something evil at the Angel Grove Power Station, I'm afraid that I am unable to see what you are seeing," Zordon said.

Kimberly clutched her head, feeling more confused than ever. "Maybe I am losing my mind," she said.

"I do not believe that for a second," Zordon

said. "Whatever Goldar is up to, we will figure it out together. In the meantime, you must go to the power station and deal with the attack."

"You're right, Zordon," Kimberly said. She then held out her Power Morpher and shouted, "IT'S MORPHIN TIME!"

Moments later, the Pink Ranger made a soaring somersault into the parking lot of the Angel Grove Power Station. She saw the Putty Patrollers circling a frightened group of station workers.

"Hey, you wanna bully someone, try bullying me," the Pink Ranger shouted.

She leaped high into the air and landed between a pair of the gray-skinned Putty Patrollers. Before they could react, she destroyed one with a melee of punches to its chest, and then took out the other with a powerful back kick to its gut.

With the Putty Patrollers focused on the Pink Ranger, the station workers made a quick escape. Once they were safe, the Pink Ranger launched into full attack mode. She took out a Putty with a spinning jump kick, the next with a walloping back-fist strike, and then flung a Putty into another hard enough to take them both out with a single blow.

The other Putty Patrollers tried to fight back, but their feeble punches and kicks were no match for the fighting skills of the Pink Ranger. Once they were all defeated, the Pink Ranger turned her attention to the bigger problem at hand.

"Time to find Goldar," she said.

Inside the power station, three levels below the ground, Goldar and Finster were busy at work. Electrical bolts crackled around Goldar while he mounted the EMP bomb to the main coil of a massive electricity generator. Finster connected a cable from the power grid into a port on the side of the EMP.

"Hurry, you fool," Goldar said. "The Pink Ranger will be here any minute. We can't risk her discovering our plan."

Finster wrenched down a coupler to make sure the cable wouldn't come loose. "This is a delicate process. Rushing could be disastrous for us," he said.

"Fine, I'll keep the Pink Ranger busy while you finish here. But this better work, or I will personally hold you responsible," Goldar threatened. He headed up a metal staircase, but only made it up one flight of stairs before he came upon the Pink Ranger, who was dashing down.

"What are you up to, Goldar?" the Pink Ranger asked.

"Look at this—first the Pink Ranger ran away from me, now she comes looking for me," Goldar teased.

"Enough with the head games. Tell me why I'm the only one who can see you," the Pink Ranger said.

"Take me to the Command Center, and I'll tell you everything," Goldar replied.

"I've got a better idea." The Pink Ranger took a fighting stance. "I give you a major butt-kicking and then I ask again." She leaped toward Goldar, and the fight was on.

Down below, Finster heard the Pink Ranger and Goldar engaged in a furious fight. With no time to spare, he finished locking down the power cable to the EMP.

"Now, my magnificent creation, it's time to get you charged up," he said, and then flicked a switch on the EMP. A sizzling surge of electricity shot through the cable, zapping Finster and sending him soaring backward into a wall.

The station's lights flickered and faded. "That may have worked a little too well," Finster groaned. He clutched his head and stumbled over to the EMP. The needle on the bomb's power gauge was flickering just above the EMPTY line.

"Success," Finster raved. "Soon my creation will knock out the Command Center and destroy every electronic device in Angel Grove."

Just then, Goldar came plummeting down the staircase and crashed into the concrete floor, as if someone had kicked him.

"Uh-oh. Looks like it's time for me to get out of here," Finster said. He then teleported away.

The Pink Ranger stomped down the stairs, holding her Power Bow. "Goldar, I've asked once. I've asked twice. I'm asking only one more time. Why am I the only one who can see you?" She then aimed her bow at Goldar.

"That's for me to know and for you to find out," Goldar said. He teleported away before the Pink Ranger could fire a shot.

The Pink Ranger grunted in frustration. She looked around the area, trying to figure out what Goldar could have been doing there, but she didn't see the EMP. "So help me, Goldar. I'm going to figure out what you're up to if it's the last thing I do," she said.

Chapter 9

Later that night, Kimberly teleported into the backyard of her home in the Angel Grove suburbs. She anxiously looked around the yard to make sure Goldar wasn't lurking anywhere.

Suddenly, the porch light popped on and the back door creaked open.

"Kimmy, what are you doing out there?" the voice of Kimberly's mother, Mrs. Hart, called out.

"Just stargazing, Mom," Kimberly muttered.

Mrs. Hart stepped out onto the porch and looked up into the sky. "I saw that strange flash of pink light again."

Kimberly knew the flash was from when she teleported into the yard—not that she could admit this to her mother. She needed to change the subject quick.

"Hey, I have good news. I advanced in the gymnastics tournament," she said.

"Oh, Kimmy, I'm so proud of you," Mrs. Hart said. She put an arm around Kimberly as they entered the house. "I'm sorry I wasn't able to be there to cheer you on. With all that's been going on at work, it's getting tougher and tougher to get time off."

"That's okay, Mom," Kimberly said. She took one last cautious look around the backyard before closing the door and locking it tight.

In the living room, Mrs. Hart turned off the television. "If you keep winning like this, you'll be off to the Pan Global Games before you know it."

"I sure hope so, Mom," Kimberly said with a smile.

"I know so," Mrs. Hart said proudly. "Now off to bed. It's late, and you've got another big day at the tournament."

Kimberly hugged her mom and headed off down the hallway. When she got to the bathroom door, her hand trembled a little as she reached inside to flick on the light switch. She took a few steps in and peeked behind the shower curtain to make sure Goldar wasn't there.

While brushing her teeth, she thought about how the next day she would be competing in both the gymnastics tournament and the *Toughest Warrior* competition. Teleporting from one location to the other would be easy enough to manage, but she wondered if she could possibly have the endurance to get through both events.

Kimberly went into her bedroom and made another nerve-racking search. First, she checked under the bed, and then inside the closet. Once satisfied Goldar wasn't waiting to jump out at her, she changed into her favorite pajamas and climbed into bed.

For the hour that followed, Kimberly tried to fall asleep, but her mind was abuzz with dreadful thoughts. What if Goldar could get into her house? What if he attacked her while she was sleeping? Or worse, what if Goldar went after her mother?

The streetlight outside the window started to rapidly flicker. Kimberly dashed over and looked outside. Streetlights were flickering all the way down the block. Then every light in the neighborhood went dark. She made another quick dash across the room and hit the light switch, but the light didn't come on.

Kimberly cautiously opened her bedroom door. "Mom, I think we're having a power blackout," she hollered, but Mrs. Hart didn't respond.

Kimberly timidly took a step into the hallway and reached down for an emergency flashlight plugged into the wall. She snapped on the light and walked to her mother's bedroom door, then shined the light into the room. Mrs. Hart was in bed, in a deep sleep.

The sound of shattering glass rang out from the far end of the house. Kimberly spun around and shined the flashlight down the dark hallway. She then heard feet scampering across the living room floor.

With a deep breath to gather her courage, she headed into the living room. She shined the flashlight around and saw a broken vase on the floor near the fireplace.

Another shattering crash came from inside the kitchen. Kimberly pressed a hand over her mouth to hold back a scream. As she walked toward the kitchen doorway, she could feel her heart pounding inside her chest. When she got up the courage to peek into the kitchen, her flashlight reflected off the eyes of a pair of Putty Patrollers that were digging through a cupboard.

The Putty Patrollers raised their hands to shield their glossy black eyes from the light. Kimberly could no longer contain her fear. She shrieked and stumbled backward onto the living room floor. The Putty Patrollers looked at one another and dashed after her.

Chapter 10

Kimberly stood quivering in the middle of her living room. Her fists were raised and ready for a fight. Two Putty Patrollers leaped out from the kitchen. "You nimrods are going to regret ever stepping foot in my house," she said.

The first Putty lurched at Kimberly. She executed a quick spinning kick, bashing it in the face. The Putty stumbled back and crashed into a bookshelf. Books and assorted knickknacks smashed to the floor. The Putty exploded into chunks of clay and vanished.

The second Putty hunched low and charged at Kimberly. It locked its arms around her waist and tried to wrestle her to the floor. Kimberly flailed with all her strength until the Putty could no longer keep a grip. She followed up with a powerful side kick, sending the brute crashing into the brick fireplace. The Putty exploded and disappeared.

Kimberly looked to the hallway, expecting to see

her mother frantically racing out of her bedroom. Luckily, Mrs. Hart had had a very long day at work, so she slept through the whole ordeal.

"Guess I'd better clean up this mess. And figure out what the heck I'm going to tell Mom," Kimberly said.

"Maybe you should tell her all about how you're the Pink Ranger," Goldar said from behind Kimberly.

Kimberly spun around and came face to face with Goldar. "This can't be happening. I must be dreaming," she said.

"This is no dream, Pink Ranger," Goldar said. "Now you have two choices. Take me to the Command Center, or I introduce myself to your precious mommy."

"If you ever so much as step foot near my mother, I will end you. You hear me, Goldar?" Kimberly said with a dangerous snarl. She threw a punch at his jaw. The hit connected, causing him to stumble, but not enough to do any serious harm.

"Your puny punch can't hurt me," Goldar teased. "Now what's it going to be?"

Kimberly knew taking Goldar to the Command Center would lead to disaster, but she also had to protect her mother. "Fine, have it your way," she said. "Just promise that after this is over, you'll never come back to my house again."

"You have my word," Goldar vowed.

Kimberly could tell Goldar was lying. She reached behind her back and pulled out her Power Morpher.

Kimberly extended a hand to Goldar. She shivered when his cold metal-gloved hand touched hers. There was no way she would take him to the Command Center, so she entered another location into her communicator watch. She then took a deep breath, held the air in her lungs, and pressed a button on the watch.

Together, Kimberly and Goldar teleported out of the house.

Seconds later, they appeared over the center of the lake at Angel Grove Park.

"What have you done, Pink Ranger?" Goldar asked as they splashed into the lake.

Kimberly began to kick at Goldar, trying to force him to release her hand as they quickly sank to the bottom. Before Kimberly could swim away, Goldar locked his arms around her. He then squeezed her tight, forcing the air out of her lungs.

Kimberly began to lose her strength and started to black out. She knew there was only one chance for her to get away from Goldar. She held out her Power Morpher and, with her last bit of air, shouted, "It's Morphin Time."

Kimberly morphed into the Pink Ranger. With a mighty outward thrust of her arms, she broke free from Goldar's grip. He tried to grab for her again, but the Pink Ranger teleported away.

Seconds later, the Pink Ranger flopped to the floor in the living room of her home. She quickly pulled off her helmet and gasped to catch her breath.

Mrs. Hart called out from her bedroom, "I woke up to a crashing noise and saw the pink flash of light again."

"It's nothing, Mom. Just go back to sleep," Kimberly replied. She then looked around at the mess of shattered glass all over the floor and let out a frustrated sigh.

Chapter 11

In the late morning, Kimberly arrived at Angel Grove Park for the *Toughest Warrior* contest. The fruit smoothie she had guzzled was keeping her awake, though she doubted it would be enough to get her through the whole day. It had taken her half the night to clean up the mess the Putty Patrollers had made at her house, and half the morning convincing her mom she had made the mess during a freak sleepwalking accident.

The park was abuzz with far more activity than Kimberly had expected. There was a carnival with game booths and thrill rides. Towering in the middle of it all was the *Toughest Warrior* obstacle course. It had ropes to climb, trapezes to swing from, balance beams to cross, rotating walkways, and collapsing bridges. There were also heavy rubber balls tied to swinging ropes designed to knock contestants into water pits.

Kimberly's communicator watch chimed. She looked around to make sure nobody was looking before she responded. "Alpha, please tell me everything is okay at my house," she said.

"A-okay so far," Alpha 5 replied. "I'm keeping a close eye on your mother."

"Thank you," Kimberly said with a sigh of relief. "And please remember to let me know when I need to be at the gymnastics competition."

"You can rely on me, Kimberly," Alpha 5 said.

Kimberly saw Sarah and her father, Jack, approaching. Jack was wearing a brightly colored tracksuit and a sweatband on his balding head.

"Good morning, Kimberly," Sarah signed. "Thank you so much for doing this. With you competing, we have a real chance to save the Center."

"Hey, don't count me out," Jack signed. "This old boy still has a few tricks left in him."

Kimberly and Sarah faked smiles.

While waiting for the contest to begin, Kimberly, Sarah, and Jack walked around the carnival. They came upon a tomato toss game. Bulk was managing the booth while Skull sat upon a pedestal, working as the human target.

"Step right up and smear the fool, if you think you can," Bulk declared. "Only one dollar."

"Yeah, smear the fool," Skull giggled.

"I would like to try," Sarah signed. "Dad, can I please? These are the guys who made fun of me yesterday."

"In that case . . ." Jack pulled out his wallet and slapped a twenty-dollar bill on the table. "I'll take a bucket."

Bulk set a large bucket of tomatoes in front of Jack. "That's what I like to see. A man willing to put his money where his mouth is," he said.

"Give it to him good," Kimberly signed to Sarah.

Sarah picked up a tomato and flung it at Skull, missing him by a long shot.

She gritted her teeth and flung another tomato, then another, and another, missing every time. Skull taunted her with goofy faces and obnoxious laughs. After going through half the bucket without success, Sarah slumped in defeat.

"Don't worry. They're not worth getting upset over," Kimberly signed.

"I'm not ready to give up," Jack said. He rolled up his sleeves and took a stance like a baseball pitcher, then flung the tomato like a pro, hitting Skull right in the face. "Did I mention I went all-state in college?" he asked with a grin.

Kimberly and Sarah cheered.

"No fair. You didn't say I'd really get hit," Skull whined to Bulk.

"Should have thought of that before you took the job," Bulk said, and laughed.

"Your job isn't done yet. I plan to get my twenty bucks' worth," Jack said. He then grabbed another tomato. For the next few minutes, Kimberly and Sarah cheered Jack on as he flung one tomato after the next, nailing Skull again and again.

Skull ducked, ran for cover, and cowered in the corner. When Bulk began mocking Skull, Jack flung tomatoes at him, too. By the time Jack was done, a crowd had gathered, and all were laughing and pointing at Bulk and Skull.

"I don't see anything funny about this," Bulk whined.

"Yeah, we're just a couple of guys trying to make a buck," Skull sobbed.

"I hope you learned your lesson," Kimberly said. "It doesn't feel too good to be laughed at."

"This is all your fault," Bulk barked at Skull.

"My fault? You said this job would be easy," Skull barked back.

They wrestled around like a pair of rowdy kids.

"Way to go, Dad," Sarah signed to Jack, and gave him a big hug.

"Yeah, Mr. Robins. You really do have some tricks left in you." Kimberly gave Jack a pat on the shoulder.

"Thanks," Jack said. Then he gripped his shoulder. "Though I might have overdone it just a bit."

"Sure you can still do the contest?" Kimberly asked.

"No problem. I just need to sit down for a bit," Jack said. He stumbled over to a bench and hunched in pain.

"I'd better go with him," Sarah signed, and then followed her father.

Kimberly's communicator chimed. She sighed, fearing this would be more bad news. "What's up, Alpha?" she asked.

"Aye-yi-yi," Alpha 5 cried. "Somebody had to drop out of the gymnastics contest, so you're up next."

"Aye-yi-yi is right," Kimberly grumbled. "The contest here starts in twenty minutes."

"It looks like you're going to have to make a choice between one or the other," Alpha 5 said gravely.

Kimberly saw Sarah rubbing Jack's shoulder. Judging by the strained look on his face, she doubted he would be able to run the course that day, or perhaps any other. It was now certain that it was up to her to save the Center.

"Alpha, I'm still going to do both," she decided.

Chapter 12

"Final call for Kimberly Ann Hart. Please report to the contest floor in one minute, or you will be disqualified," an announcer said over the intercom of the Angel Grove Youth Center.

Kimberly hurried out of the dressing room, after having made a quick change into her leotard. Careful to assure herself that nobody was watching, she pulled out her Morpher and removed the Power Coin. She then safely tucked the coin inside her leotard, and hid the Morpher at the bottom of her backpack.

On the intercom, the announcer said, "Sorry, folks, it appears Kimberly Hart will not be competing today."

"Wait, I'm here," Kimberly called out, rushing toward the check-in table.

The manager at the table gave Kimberly a disapproving glare. "I was a half second from crossing your name off the list. If this happens again, you won't be so lucky," she said.

Kimberly nodded and thanked the manager.

While walking over to the balance beam, Kimberly did a few quick stretches. She usually would have done her full warm-up routine, but she didn't want to upset the judges any further. She then stuffed her backpack under a nearby bench and took her starting position.

Kimberly took a deep breath and sprinted toward a springboard. In a single bound, she somersaulted high into the air. When she landed on the balance beam, a glimmering gold light caught her eye. It was Goldar, standing on the opposite end of the beam.

"We meet again, Pink Ranger," Goldar said.

Kimberly was so startled that she almost fell from the beam. She knew this would cost her a minor point deduction, but not nearly as much as it would have cost her if she had fallen. Of course, that was the least of her problems at the moment.

"Hope you're ready to play some more," Goldar said. He started to wildly swing his sword. Kimberly perfectly executed a series of dazzling backflips, half-twists, and split leaps to dodge the strikes and stay on the beam.

The audience cheered with great excitement. Based on their reaction, Kimberly was certain that they couldn't see Goldar. She decided it was time to turn the situation to her advantage.

"Now it's my turn to play," she said.

She unleashed a melee of high kicks, bashing Goldar in the stomach, chest, and face. Then she did a triple spinning jump kick, landing three strikes to his jaw. Goldar grunted and dizzily stumbled backward.

The crowd again cheered excitedly. Kimberly knew she was showing them something they had never seen before. She also knew it was time to perform her dismount and finish the routine.

"I'm going to make you suffer for that," Goldar wailed.

"Not before I make you suffer," Kimberly said with gritted teeth. She leaped high and gave Goldar a double front kick, then twisted into a backflip. Goldar soared away and crashed face-first into the ground.

When Kimberly landed on the beam, she performed two back handsprings and then dismounted with a double backflip twist. The crowd cheered wildly when she stuck a perfect landing.

As Kimberly wheezed to catch her breath, she

looked around to make sure Goldar was gone. Then the familiar chime of her communicator watch sounded from inside her backpack.

As much as Kimberly wanted to wait around to find out her score, she didn't have a moment to spare. She scooped up her backpack and raced over to the dressing room. Once inside, she took the communicator from her backpack and strapped it to her wrist.

"What's up, Alpha?" she asked.

"Aye-yi-yi. I don't mean to rush you, but they just announced you're up next at the *Toughest Warrior* contest," Alpha 5 said frantically.

"Not already," Kimberly said with a sigh. She made a quick change back into her tracksuit, and slipped her Power Coin into her pocket.

"I'm sorry, Kimberly. Nobody will blame you if you back out now," Alpha 5 replied.

"I can't do that. The kids at the Center are counting on me," Kimberly said. She peeked out into the dressing room to make sure nobody was around. She then tapped her communicator and was gone in a flash.

Chapter 13

Back at Angel Grove Park, Kimberly raced through the crowded carnival to get to the *Toughest Warrior* obstacle course. By the time she made it to the check-in desk, she was wheezing to catch her breath.

Sarah raced over to greet Kimberly. "I'm so happy you're still here. We thought maybe you had changed your mind," she signed.

"I would never back out on a promise," Kimberly replied. She looked around for Jack. "What happened to your dad?"

Sarah grimaced and pointed toward the obstacle course. Kimberly's heart sank when she saw Jack was at the midpoint of the course, hunched over in exhaustion, and limping on a twisted ankle. He tried to leap to a rotating platform, but missed and plummeted into a pool far below.

Sarah sulked in disappointment. "I tried to talk him out of it, but we thought you had left, so he felt like he didn't have a choice," she signed.

Kimberly sighed, feeling awfully guilty.

The show manager approached Kimberly. "Listen up, Hart, I'm only saying this once. You will be disqualified if you so much as take one step onto the course before the starting buzzer sounds. And if you want to advance to the next round, you must complete every challenge and hit the big red button in under ten minutes. Do you understand these rules?" he asked.

Kimberly nodded an affirmative. She then handed her backpack to Sarah. "Please keep this safe. Keep it close to you," she signed.

"I promise," Sarah signed back.

In the Moon Palace, Rita Repulsa was spying on Kimberly through her telescope. Her eyes widened with wicked delight when she saw Kimberly had given her backpack to Sarah. "Oh, this is just too perfect," Rita said. "That foolish Pink Ranger has left her backpack in the hands of her mousy little friend."

Rita turned to Goldar, who was standing by her side. "Get down there and grab the girl and the backpack while the Pink Ranger is distracted with that ridiculous obstacle course."

"How would getting the Pink Ranger's backpack help us, my queen?" Goldar asked, scratching his head in confusion.

Rita bashed Goldar with her staff. "The Pink Ranger's Morpher is inside the backpack. No Morpher means no morphing."

Goldar raised a fist, now understanding her meaning. "Yes. Without her Morpher, the Pink Ranger couldn't hope to stop us."

"And with you holding her little friend hostage, she'll have no choice but to do whatever you say," Rita said.

"And what will I say she has to do, my queen?" Goldar asked curiously.

Rita groaned in irritation. "Take you to the Command Center. With her help, you'll be able to get inside without being detected. Zordon wouldn't see you coming until it's too late." Rita again struck Goldar with her staff. "Now get out of my sight and don't you dare fail me again."

. . .

Kimberly anxiously stood waiting on the starting platform of the obstacle course. Her nerves were so rattled, she didn't hear the starting buzzer sound. If not for the crowd screaming for her to go, she might have stood there all day.

The first obstacle was an ascending balance beam spanning a water pit. Kimberly hurried across with effortless ease. She then leaped across three rotating platforms, while narrowly evading swinging ropes that had large rubber balls hooked to the ends.

Next, she climbed a rope while water jets blasted down on her from above. At the top, she swung on a trapeze to cross a wide chasm. After that, she leapfrogged across six floating platforms. Then she raced across the collapsing bridge, narrowly making it to the other side.

When she reached the midpoint of the course where Jack had fallen, she glanced up at the clock. She was thrilled to see that only four minutes had passed. It seemed that six minutes would be more than enough time to reach the end.

Just as she was about to leap to a spinning platform, a blazing flash of light forced her to stop and shield her eyes. When her vision came back into focus, she was startled to see a Putty Patroller standing on the spinning platform. Then she looked up and saw there were more of the dim-witted brutes swarming all throughout the remainder of the course.

With a frustrated sigh, Kimberly grumbled, "Well, isn't this just spiffy!"

Chapter 14

Kimberly gave a hard glare to the Putty Patroller on the spinning platform. "I don't know why you witless jerks would attack me here, but I'm not about to let you mess up my chance to save the Center," she said.

She made a leaping dive roll and landed on the spinning platform, then popped up behind the Putty. With a quick side kick, she sent the brute splashing down into the water pit below.

In the spectator area, Sarah and Jack sat among a cheering crowd. Sarah was still holding Kimberly's backpack. The sudden appearance of the Putty Patrollers had everyone bewildered with excitement.

"Is this part of the contest?" Sarah signed to Jack.

"If it is, I'm sure glad I tanked before those things showed up," Jack replied.

. . .

Kimberly leaped across a series of five rising and falling platforms. On each platform, she dodged, jumped over, and shoved a Putty Patroller out of her way.

When she reached a swaying rope bridge, she saw three more of the brutes were blocking her way. As she started to cross, the first Putty locked its burly arms around her. She thrashed around to break free and sent the Putty tumbling.

The crowd cheered excitedly.

The second Putty tried to knock Kimberly off the bridge, but she ducked down.

The third Putty flailed its arms wildly, trying to bash Kimberly. She skillfully placed her toe in its path, causing the Putty to trip and stumble out of sight.

In the spectator area, Jack and the rest of the crowd stood up and cheered. Sarah could tell by the distressed expression on Kimberly's face that something about this just wasn't right. Sarah suddenly noticed a trail of large footsteps were appearing in the nearby grass, as if an invisible man was walking through the crowd, and he seemed to be heading her way.

Sarah tapped her father on the shoulder. "Dad, I think we should get out of here. Something weird is happening," she signed.

"Sure, honey, just as soon as Kimberly is done," he replied, and turned his attention back to the obstacle course.

Kimberly was clawing her way up a rock-climbing wall. She looked down and saw two Putty Patrollers climbing up after her. The first Putty reached up and tried to grab her leg, but Kimberly kicked it hard enough to send it tumbling down.

The second Putty got a grip on Kimberly's ankle. She had to hold on with all her might as the Putty pulled and pulled. With a strained grunt, Kimberly pulled her leg upward, and then thrust it downward. The Putty lost its grip and plummeted away.

Right as Kimberly clawed her way to the top of the rock wall, a buzzer sounded, indicating she had two minutes remaining to complete the course. She worried that her chance of qualifying for the next round was slipping away.

"If I'm going to finish in time, I need to shift into

overdrive," Kimberly said through gritted teeth.

She broke into a sprint. She executed a spinning jump kick, sending a Putty soaring away, then double-punched another, knocking it out of its senses. With most of the Putty Patrollers now defeated, she was clear to deal with the toughest part of the course.

Chapter 15

In the spectator area, Sarah fearfully watched the footsteps of the invisible stalker that were still heading her way. "Dad, please, we have to go," she signed to Jack.

"We will. Just as soon as Kimberly is finished," Jack signed in reply.

Sarah's heart raced with fright when she saw the footsteps of the invisible stalker had stopped directly next to her. With a trembling hand, she reached out, hoping against hope that nothing was actually there. She cried out a frightened squeal when her hand touched something cold and metallic.

"I see you, but you can't see me," Goldar said— not that Sarah could hear him.

Goldar reached out and grabbed Sarah's arm. The feeling of his cold metal glove made her screech even louder. She frantically yanked away from his grip and dashed away, still holding tight to Kimberly's backpack.

"Hey, get back here," Goldar said as he furiously stomped off after Sarah.

"Sarah, what's wrong?" Jack called out, and followed after her.

A one-minute warning buzzer sounded.

Kimberly was struggling to climb a rope ladder that led to the final platform. Water jets blasted her from every direction, making it all the more challenging. As if that wasn't bad enough, two Putty Patrollers were climbing up after her.

With every rung upward, Kimberly could feel her muscles getting weaker. Her fingers ached with fatigue. Outright exhaustion was setting in. She looked down and saw the Putty Patrollers were closing in.

For a brief instant, Kimberly thought about just giving up, but then she realized that doing so would be the same as letting Goldar win, and the Center would suffer for it.

Kimberly dug down deep and found one last spurt of strength. It was just enough to pull herself up over the ledge and roll onto the platform. She had to gasp for every breath as she stumbled to her feet.

The final obstacle was a trapeze spanning a twenty-foot gap. A dozen heavy sandbags were swinging back and forth. Her timing needed to be perfect or she would be knocked off and lose the contest.

She then noticed the Putty Patrollers were climbing up onto the platform. With only thirty seconds remaining on the clock, there was no time to fight them off.

Kimberly had to go now.

Down on the ground, Sarah raced through the crowd. She looked back over her shoulder but she was unable to see that Goldar was chasing her and gaining on her quickly. It didn't take long for him to close the distance and grab her from behind.

"Got you now," Goldar said. He flung Sarah over his shoulder. Before she even knew what was happening, Goldar teleported them away.

Seconds later, Jack frantically raced by, clueless about what had just happened to Sarah.

. . .

Kimberly held tight to the trapeze. She watched the swaying sandbags, waiting for the perfect moment to go. Then the ten-second warning buzzer sounded. The Putty Patrollers rolled up onto the platform. Just as they tried to grab Kimberly, she swung out on the trapeze.

Soaring across the chasm, Kimberly passed between the swinging sandbags, missing each one by inches. When she reached the other side, she let go of the trapeze and flew forward. With only one second left, she reached out and smacked her palm on the big red button. The victory horn sounded. The crowd cheered excitedly.

Kimberly flopped down into a pit of rubber mats. She took a deep breath of relief and pulled herself up to her feet. No sooner than she got her balance, her communicator chimed. It was Alpha 5, and he was calling to inform her that she needed to get to the Command Center right away.

Chapter 16

When Kimberly arrived at the Command Center, Alpha 5 nearly knocked her over. He was running in a frantic tizzy from one control console to another, flicking switches, turning dials, and checking data readouts.

"Aye-yi-yi, this is worse than I thought," Alpha 5 said as he hurried over to the viewing globe.

"Alpha, what's wrong?" Kimberly asked as she stepped up next to him.

"The entire Angel Grove power grid is failing," Alpha 5 replied. "There are blackouts happening all over the city." On the viewing globe, they saw Downtown Angel Grove was in chaos. Traffic lights were out, and emergency crews were dealing with multiple car wrecks.

Kimberly looked up at Zordon. "Do you think whatever Goldar was doing at the power station has something to do with the blackouts?"

"We have been unable to determine the cause

of the blackouts, but it's a good chance Goldar is responsible," Zordon said.

"Then I'd better get to the power station and figure out what's going on," Kimberly replied.

"I'm afraid there is another pressing matter," Zordon said. "Your friend Sarah is being held hostage by Putty Patrollers at Angel Grove Beach."

On the viewing globe, Kimberly saw Sarah at the beach. She was cowering in the sand with the backpack within arm's reach. Goldar and a squad of Putty Patrollers were swarming around her.

"Oh no. This is bad. Like, really bad," Kimberly said.

"Agreed. You must morph into the Pink Ranger and get to Angel Grove Beach right away," Zordon said.

Kimberly sighed in distress. "That's the problem. I gave my backpack to Sarah for safekeeping, and my Morpher is inside of it."

"Aye-yi-yi," said Alpha 5. "If Goldar finds out, he would stop at nothing to get the Morpher away from Sarah."

"It is imperative that you retrieve the Morpher and rescue your friend Sarah," Zordon said.

"But how can I do that if I can't morph?" Kimberly nervously asked.

"You have the skills, Kimberly. And I'll be here if you need anything," Zordon replied. "May the Power protect you."

In a flash of pink light, Kimberly teleported to Angel Grove Beach. She took cover behind a boulder near the cliff wall and cautiously peeked out. Fifty yards away, she saw that Goldar and the Putty Patrollers were still holding Sarah hostage.

Kimberly strained to come up with a plan to get her Morpher back without Goldar seeing her, but she just couldn't think of anything. Just then, she heard the unmistakable voices of Bulk and Skull speaking from somewhere nearby.

She cautiously crept along the cliff and rounded the corner of a rocky alcove. The dim-witted duo were wearing old diving suits made of thick rubber and had round iron helmets. The suits reminded Kimberly of alien invaders from an old monster movie she had once seen.

As much as Kimberly hated even speaking to Bulk and Skull, their suits gave her an idea that could be just crazy enough to work.

"Hey, guys, can we talk for a sec?" Kimberly asked as she approached them.

Bulk and Skull squealed in unison and spun around.

"Kimberly, this isn't what it looks like," Bulk said.

"Yeah, and whatever you think it looks like ain't what it looks like, so forget you saw anything," Skull said.

"I seriously don't care what you two are doing," Kimberly replied.

"You won't be saying that after we find the lost treasure of Bobo the Pirate King," Skull said proudly. He held up an old parchment treasure map. "According to this map I bought off my cousin Vinnie, the treasure is buried out there somewhere, and we're going to find it."

"Ixnay on the treasure-aye, you bonehead-aye," Bulk said.

"Don't you call me a bonehead-aye, you nimrod-aye," Skull replied.

They started to shove and slap at one another.

"Stop it. I don't care about your dumb treasure," Kimberly said with a long sigh. "I just need a favor from you guys."

Bulk held up a finger. "First of all, there's nothing dumb about treasure."

Skull held up two fingers. "Second of all, when is the last time you ever saw us help anyone with anything?"

Kimberly knew Skull was right. "Fine, I'll make you a deal. You help me, and I won't tell anyone about your treasure."

"Yikes! I knew she was going to say that." Bulk gave Skull a shove. "This is why you're supposed to ixnay."

"You never told me we were ixnaying," Skull whined.

Kimberly waited impatiently while Bulk and Skull debated in whispering voices that she could clearly hear.

"What do you need us to do?" Bulk asked.

"There's a bunch of big gray guys on the beach in a dopey costumes," Kimberly began. "I need you to distract them for a bit. Then, and only then, will I keep your secret."

"Fine, but we have one condition," Bulk said.

"When this is done, we both get to go on a date with you," Skull said.

"Absolutely never," Kimberly replied.

Bulk and Skull frowned in disappointment.

Chapter 17

Sarah cowered in fear as she watched Goldar's footsteps forming in the sand while he paced around her, but she still couldn't see him.

"Pink Ranger, I'm waiting for you," Goldar shouted. "Come out, come out, wherever you are."

The Putty Patrollers began jabbering in a panic. Bulk and Skull were approaching, wearing their dive suits and metal helmets. Strands of wet seaweed dangled all over them.

"We are intergalactic invaders from the planet Monsteria," Bulk said.

"We seek to join you in your quest to take over the world, or whatever you're doing here," Skull said.

"Seize those fools," Goldar ordered, and knocked Sarah into the sand. The Putty Patrollers grabbed Bulk and Skull.

Skull whispered to Bulk, "What are we supposed to do now?"

"How should I know? Kimberly just said to distract them," Bulk whispered back.

Near the cliff wall, Kimberly peeked out over the rocks and saw the Putty Patrollers were now swarming around Bulk and Skull, and Goldar was stalking their way. She then noticed Sarah's attention was also focused on what was happening. The backpack was just a couple of feet behind her.

If there was a chance to recover her Morpher without being noticed, she had to act now, Kimberly thought. With a deep breath to calm her nerves, she leaped out from behind the rocks and raced toward the backpack.

Goldar stood facing Bulk and Skull. He tapped his finger on the amulet three times, temporarily disabling its mystical effect so they could see him. "What do you want, and who sent you?" he asked.

Bulk's and Skull's eyes widened with terror.

"W-who sent us?" Bulk asked, his voice trembling. He noticed Kimberly grabbing the backpack and then dashing away toward the boulders. "We, ah, were sent here by the supreme leader of our faraway alien world," he said.

"Yeah," Skull nervously added. "Now take us to your leader . . . or else."

Goldar grabbed Skull by the helmet. "I have a better idea. Get out of my sight before I squash you like a pair of bugs."

Bulk saw Kimberly was crawling back behind the rocks near the sea cliff. "That is a very fair offer," he whimpered.

"Good luck with your plot to rule the world," Skull said, weeping like a baby.

Bulk and Skull stumbled away, yelping.

Goldar stomped back over toward Sarah. "Now, where is that wretched Pink Ranger?" he shouted.

Behind the rocks where Kimberly had been hiding, there was a shimmering flash of pink light. Then the Pink Ranger somersaulted through the air and landed near Goldar. "Let the girl go," she demanded.

"Putty Patrollers, seize her," Goldar ordered.

The Putties flocked around her, and the fight was on. Sarah watched in wide-eyed astonishment as the Pink Ranger punched, kicked, flipped, and twisted around, quickly taking out the dim-witted thugs.

Once they were all defeated, the Pink Ranger pulled out her Power Bow, loaded an arrow, and aimed it at Goldar. He was still clutching Sarah tight in one arm.

"I'm not going to warn you again, Goldar," the Pink Ranger demanded.

"Actually, I was just going to say the same thing to you." Goldar tightened his grip on Sarah. "Now take me to the Command Center, or else," he said grimly.

The Pink Ranger couldn't risk taking a shot with Sarah in the line of fire. "Fine. Let her go, and you can have whatever you want," she said, lowering her bow.

"You think I'm stupid enough to trust you again? First give me the coin, then the girl goes free," Goldar replied.

With no other choice, the Pink Ranger dropped the Power Bow in the sand. She slowly walked toward Goldar, trying to think up a way out of this mess.

Just when all seemed lost, a rock hit Goldar in the back. He turned right as another rock soared his way. He looked down by the water and saw Bulk and Skull throwing the rocks.

"And why exactly are we doing this?" Skull asked Bulk.

"I'll explain later," Bulk replied. "We're safe behind this boulder. Just keep flinging."

With Goldar distracted, Sarah wiggled free from his grip. Once she was clear, the Pink Ranger leaped back and picked up her Power Bow. She then took aim at Goldar and fired. The arrow hit his armored chest and exploded with enough force to knock him off his feet.

The Pink Ranger loaded another arrow and took aim at Goldar. "Give it up, Goldar. It's over," she said.

"Wrong again, Pink Ranger." Goldar laughed wickedly and then vanished in a golden flash.

The Pink Ranger dashed to Sarah. She almost used sign language to ask Sarah if she was okay, but then realized that doing so might give away who she really was. The Pink Ranger instead gave a thumbs-up. Sarah replied by doing the same.

"Hey, Pink Ranger," Bulk called out as he and Skull strutted her way.

"Thank you for your help, citizens," the Pink Ranger said.

"We don't want your thanks. You owe us a big

favor for saving your tail from whatever that thing was," Bulk said.

Skull pulled out the treasure map and showed it to the Pink Ranger. "There's treasure out there, and we're looking for it. You must have some kind of super scanning device at your secret Ranger base that can figure out where it's hidden."

The Pink Ranger sighed. "Fine, I'll help you, but you have to do one more thing for me," she said. "Take the girl back to Angel Grove Park. That's the deal. Take it or leave it."

Bulk and Skull deviously smiled. "Deal," they said.

"Then I'll contact you soon. And you'd better be nice to the girl or the deal is off," the Pink Ranger said.

Then she teleported away.

Chapter 18

At the Moon Palace, Rita bashed Goldar with her staff. "Fools. I'm surrounded by fools," she shrilled. "You not only failed to get the Pink Ranger's Power Coin, you allowed those idiots Bulk and Skull to see you."

"Why does that matter?" Goldar asked.

"You were supposed to make the Pink Ranger think she was going cuckoo because she was the only one who could see you, but now she must know something else is going on. So I have to come up with a new plan," Rita shrilled.

Finster nervously approached Rita. "My queen, the EMP is far from being fully charged. If the Pink Ranger were to discover it, all of our plans will be ruined."

"You think I don't know that?" Rita said, and shoved Finster aside. She went over to her telescope and looked at Downtown Angel Grove. She grinned with devious delight at the sight of the city still in chaos from the random power outages.

Then she angled the telescope toward Angel Grove Park. The *Toughest Warrior* contest was still in full swing. "We need to find another way to keep the Pink Ranger off balance, and I know exactly what we're going to do," she said.

Rita turned away from the telescope. "Goldar, get over here." He hurried over and knelt before her.

"What is your new plan, my queen?" Goldar asked.

Rita touched the tip of her staff to the amulet around Goldar's neck. A spark of magical power zapped from the staff, causing the amulet to glow with a mesmerizing swirl of pink light. "The new plan is the old plan, with a devious twist. Now when you're near the Pink Ranger, the amulet is going to really scramble her mind."

"I will not fail you again, my queen," Goldar vowed.

At the Command Center, the Pink Ranger pulled off her helmet. She sighed when she saw the clock over the console had just passed the twenty-four-hour mark, meaning a full day remained until the other Rangers were due to return.

"Aye-yi-yi," Alpha 5 yelped. "You look exhausted, Kimberly."

"Agreed," Zordon said. "It would do you well to return home for some much-needed rest."

Kimberly shook her head. "Maybe later. I still need to figure out what Goldar was up to at the power station."

"I'll handle that," Alpha 5 said. "I can teleport in and out without anyone knowing."

"I'm not so sure that's a good idea," Kimberly said uneasily. "If Goldar were to discover you there—"

Alpha 5 interrupted, "Don't you worry, I can handle myself." He started doing karate chops with his hands. "I'll give that Goldar a *hi-yah* and a *he-cha*!"

Kimberly looked skeptically up to Zordon. "If anything happens, promise to call me right away."

"You have my word, Kimberly," Zordon promised. "Now please get some rest."

"I'll try," Kimberly said. "But first, I need to make sure Sarah is safe."

At Angel Grove Park, Bulk and Skull were in guard duty mode. They stood with their arms folded across their chests and wore dark sunglasses. Sarah stood wedged between them, trying to figure out how to get away.

"How much longer do we gotta watch this girl?" Skull asked Bulk.

"For as long as we have to," Bulk replied.

"Sarah! Oh, thank goodness," Jack called out as he frantically dashed their way.

Bulk and Skull pumped up their chests and blocked Jack.

"Sorry, sir, we can't let you near the girl without proper authorization," Bulk said.

"We're on official orders from the Pink Ranger," said Skull.

"I'm her father. That's all the authorization you need," Jack said, and pushed around them. "Now get lost or I'll call security."

Bulk and Skull raised their hands and walked away.

Jack signed to Sarah, "I was looking all over for you. Where have you been?"

"It's a long story, Dad, but I am okay," Sarah replied.

"Sarah, there you are." Kimberly raced over and hugged her.

"Kimberly, it was so amazing. A big metal monster took me away, but the Pink Ranger came and saved me," Sarah signed.

Kimberly did her best to act surprised. "Wow. That is amazing. You'll have to tell me all about it."

"Me too," Jack said a bit skeptically. "But it will have to wait until later. Kimberly needs to get moving. The second round of the contest starts in ten minutes."

Kimberly sighed. "I thought with all the power outages, the contest would be canceled."

"These are Hollywood people. They bring their own power generators," Jack replied. "Remember, if you win today, you'll go to the final round tomorrow."

Sarah noticed how exhausted Kimberly was. "If you're too tired, nobody will hold it against you if you back out," she signed.

Kimberly considered this, but again reminded herself of the importance of saving the Center. "I'll be fine. Just give me a few minutes to warm up," she said.

"You're the best, Kimberly. I know you can do it," Jack said. He patted her on the shoulder and walked away.

Chapter 19

High up on the starting platform of the *Toughest Warrior* obstacle course, Kimberly stood waiting to start her run. She felt so tired that it took every bit of her willpower just to keep her eyes from flickering shut. This was by far the most exhausted she had ever been—and the day was far from over.

By the time the start buzzer sounded, Kimberly had nodded off. Her eyes snapped open with a startled fright. As she took off running across the first balance beam, she reminded herself that she had to finish the course in eight minutes instead of ten like the last time.

For the first two minutes, Kimberley did great. She nimbly climbed, leaped, and swung her way through the daunting obstacles. The situation took a bad turn when she reached a series of five rotating platforms and saw a copy of Goldar standing on each one. Kimberly rubbed her eyes to make sure that what she was seeing was real.

"We meet again, Pink Ranger," the five Goldars said together.

Kimberly refused to let Goldar's tricks stop her from finishing the course. She leaped to the first rotating platform and swung her fist at Goldar. It passed right through him and he disappeared.

"Missed me," Goldar taunted. "Want to try again?"

Kimberly gritted her teeth and jumped to the second platform, then the third, then the fourth, and finally the fifth. Each time, she tried to hit the Goldars, and each time they vanished from sight.

"You'll have to be faster than that," the Goldars mocked.

Then copies of Goldar appeared all throughout the course. Kimberly continued onward, doing her best to ignore his repeated attempts to stop her. He leaped in her way, roared in her face, charged at her head-on, taunted her with wicked laughter, and even made terrifying threats. Through it all, Kimberly stayed tough and pushed onward.

With only three minutes remaining to finish the course, Kimberly began to slow from exhaustion. Her muscles ached and she could hardly catch her breath.

The climb up the rock wall nearly did her in, but she refused to quit.

The one-minute warning buzzer sounded just as Kimberly rolled up onto the final platform. She pulled to her feet, but her legs felt so wobbly, she could hardly stand. Then she gripped the trapeze that would carry her across the chasm to the end of the course.

Just as she was timing out her maneuver, things went from bad to worse. The sandbags vanished and in their place, Goldars appeared. She gasped in terror at the sight of a dozen Goldars swinging on the ropes. Some were roaring and others were laughing wickedly.

With only seconds remaining, and no chance of timing out a clear path, Kimberly decided to just go for it. As she soared across the chasm, the Goldars swatted and smacked at her from every direction. The trapeze started to spin out of control.

Kimberly lost her grip and went wildly whirling into the air. Just when she thought all was lost, she crashed right into the big red button. The victory siren sounded. The crowd erupted with cheers. Kimberly had done it again.

For a lingering moment she lay on the platform,

rapidly gasping to catch her breath. She took comfort in knowing she was now one step closer to saving the Center.

It took every bit of energy Kimberly had left just to get to her feet. She gave a victory wave to the cheering crowd and then started down the stairs to exit the course. Just then, the familiar chime of her communicator watch sounded.

She let out a frustrated sigh and then responded, "What's up, Alpha?"

"I don't know how to tell you this," Alpha 5 said timidly. "It seems you're due at the final round of the gymnastics tournament in only fifteen minutes."

Kimberly slumped in defeat. She thought of how it would be so much easier to just give this all up and go home to get some sleep. She also knew how disappointed she would be in herself upon waking the next day. With this thought in mind, she decided it would be better to try, and risk failing, than to not try at all.

Chapter 20

When Kimberly arrived at the Angel Grove Youth Center, she was surprised to see that the gymnastics tournament was now taking place in the parking lot. It seemed the constant power blackouts had made it impossible to continue inside the building.

With only minutes to spare, she raced to a vendor's booth to buy a new leotard. Goldar had dumped her other one on the beach when he searched her backpack. If this wasn't enough of an inconvenience, the only size the vendor had available was two sizes too large for Kimberly.

Through a handheld megaphone, the announcer called out, "Next up on the vault, Kimberly Hart."

As Kimberly walked out onto the tournament floor, she noticed a few spectators were pointing at her and giggling. She knew it was because of her oversize leotard, but she was too tired to let it bother her.

Kimberly was relieved that she only had to

perform three vaults to complete the tournament. She took her position at the starting point and then sprinted toward a springboard, planted her hands on the vault, and launched into a double backflip. While in midflight, she caught a glimpse of Goldar standing in the exact spot she planned to land.

"You'll never escape me," Goldar snarled.

Kimberly squealed, expecting to land right on him, but he vanished as soon as her feet touched the mat. Somehow, she kept her wits and perfectly stuck the landing. The crowd cheered. A few of the other competitors even praised her effort and gave her high fives.

Kimberly's legs wobbled as she made her way back to the starting point. She couldn't help but wonder if she was really seeing Goldar or if her mind was playing tricks on her. She took a deep breath and prepared for her second vault. This time, Goldar appeared directly in front of the springboard.

"Catch me if you can," Goldar teased.

Kimberly suddenly became spellbound when she saw the pink mystical light swirling in Goldar's amulet. It took every bit of willpower she had to shake it off. With gritted teeth, she glared into

Goldar's eyes and dashed forward, uncertain if she was going to pass through him or crash into him head-on.

Just as before, Goldar vanished. The fear of the encounter got Kimberly's adrenaline so high, she executed the highest vault of her life. When she hit the ground, the crowd stood and raved over her success. Even the judges were impressed.

Wheezing to catch her breath, Kimberly ambled back over to the starting point. The adrenaline rush of the last vault was fading fast. She needed to get the third vault done quickly, or she was going to drop from exhaustion.

Right as she was about to start her run, she suddenly felt someone's hot breath on the back of her neck.

"Just one more to go," Goldar whispered into her ear.

Kimberly screeched and took off in a sprint. She jumped onto the springboard and hurled over the vault. Her body spiraled around so many times, even the judges couldn't keep count.

The instant her feet landed on the mat, Kimberly sprung into a fighting stance. Her muscles twitched and trembled. She looked around in every direction, but Goldar was gone.

It wasn't until several of her competitors raced over with their hands raised to high-five her that she realized the judges had awarded her a perfect score. The contest was over, and there was no doubt in anyone's mind that Kimberly had won the day.

Chapter 21

Later that evening, Kimberly lay sprawled out on her bed. A dozen flickering candles lit her room. She gazed with great pride at the gold medal she'd earned in the gymnastics tournament. The win guaranteed her a shot to compete at the national level, and perhaps one day she would go all the way to the Pan Global Games.

The door cracked open and Mrs. Hart peeked inside. "Hey there, superstar. What's with all the candles?" she asked.

Kimberly strained to sit upright. "I got tired of the lights going out every five minutes," she said.

"I'm sure the city will have this power thing figured out soon." Mrs. Hart sat on the bed next to Kimberly. "Can I get you anything? You hardly touched your dinner," she said.

Kimberly shook her head. "I don't think I have the strength left to chew," she replied.

"Okay, but I'm cooking up a victory feast in the morning, and I expect you to eat yourself full," Mrs. Hart said.

"Sounds great, Mom." Kimberly smiled warmly and hugged her mother.

"You make me so proud, Kimmy," Mrs. Hart said. She walked around the room putting out the candles. "Now get some sleep. Tomorrow is a school day."

Kimberly sighed. "I almost forgot. I still have a history test to study for."

"You'll do fine on that test. You always do," Mrs. Hart said. She put out the last candle and closed the door as she exited, leaving the room in pitch-black darkness.

Kimberly quickly opened the nightstand drawer and took out a flashlight. She flicked it on and shined the light around the room, making sure Goldar wasn't around. The fear she felt reminded her of when she was a little girl and thought a monster lived in her closet. *The big difference now is that there really could be one in there*, she thought.

She fought the urge to fall asleep, but soon she could no longer keep her eyes open. As she drifted into slumber, the flashlight faded out. No more than a minute passed before she heard the sound of her closet door creaking open.

"Wake up, Kimberly," a voice whispered.

Kimberly snapped upright and grabbed the flashlight. She flicked the power switch several times, only to discover that the batteries were dead. "Mom, is that you?" she asked.

"Your mommy can't help you now, Pink Ranger," Goldar said from somewhere in the room.

Kimberly tapped her communicator. "Alpha 5, please come in," she said urgently. She waited for a response, but heard only static.

"Your friends can't help you now," Goldar said. Just beyond the end of her bed, a pink light glimmered through the darkness.

"This has to be a dream," Kimberly said. She stumbled to her feet, holding her hands out defensively. "What do you want from me, Goldar?"

"To help me destroy Zordon and the other Rangers," Goldar said. "Then, if you're lucky, I'll make you my apprentice."

"No way. I'll never betray my friends for you," Kimberly said.

Goldar grabbed Kimberly's arm. Her eyes

widened when she saw his face illuminated in pink mystical light. "You don't have a choice, Pink Ranger," Goldar said.

Kimberly fought with all her might to pull away from his crushing grip. "Let go of me," she screamed.

When Kimberly finally pulled free, she toppled backward, and in a blink, she flopped down into a wooden chair. A rush of morning light forced her to shield her eyes. When her vision came into focus, she realized she was now sitting at the table in her kitchen. Sprawled out across the table was a savory feast of muffins, scrambled eggs, and crispy bacon.

"Who is Goldar?" Mrs. Hart asked as she entered from the other room. She then sat in the chair opposite Kimberly.

Kimberly struggled to respond, still confused over how she had gotten there. Even more baffling, she was dressed and ready to go to school. "What day is it?" she asked.

"You feeling okay, Kimmy?" Mrs. Hart asked. She pressed a hand to Kimberly's forehead, checking her for a fever. "You don't feel hot."

"Mom, I'm fine," Kimberly said. She poured a cup of orange juice and downed it in a single gulp. "I just haven't been sleeping much this week."

"In that case, you should skip competing on that crazy game show tonight. You keep pushing this hard, you're going to make yourself sick," Mrs. Hart said.

"Mom, I'll be fine. Trust me," Kimberly said. She hastily stood up to exit. "I need to get going."

"No, you need to eat and get your strength up," Mrs. Hart said. She gestured for Kimberly to sit down. "I mean it. Mother's orders."

Chapter 22

At Angel Grove High School, Kimberly snapped awake in her fourth-period history classroom. For half the day she had been walking around in a weary daze, hardly able to keep her mind focused. She glanced down at her desk and sighed when she saw her midterm exam was only half complete.

"Welcome back, Miss Hart," said her teacher, Mr. Johnson, from his desk in the front of the classroom.

"I'm sorry, I was just—" Kimberly paused, too frazzled to think up an excuse.

Mr. Johnson cleared his throat. "The correct answer is that you were sleeping in class, and it won't happen again."

"You're right, Mr. Johnson. I'm sorry," Kimberly said with a sigh. She looked down at her exam paper and read the next question. Her eyes were so tired she had to strain to make out the words.

She then noticed the four empty seats where the other Rangers usually sat. Zordon didn't normally allow Power Rangers business to interfere with their schoolwork, but they had already made arrangements to make up their assignments.

"Eyes on your exam, Miss Hart," Mr. Johnson said.

"But I wasn't—" Kimberly quivered in fear when she saw Goldar was now sitting at Mr. Johnson's desk.

"Looks like you're going to get detention," Goldar said.

As Goldar started walking toward Kimberly, she looked around at the other students. They were all focused on their test and unaware of what was happening. The pink light swirling around in Goldar's amulet caught her eye. Kimberly tried with all her will to look away from the amulet, but it had a powerful grip on her mind.

"Stay away from me. I'm warning you," she said.

"And if I don't, then what? You'll run away screaming like a frightened little girl?" Goldar asked. The pink light reflected in Kimberly's mesmerized eyes. "Now, Pink Ranger, you will help me destroy Zordon," he said.

Kimberly gritted her teeth, refusing to accept this notion. "I will never do that, and you can't make me," she shouted, and then leaped to her feet with her fists ready for a fight.

"Miss Hart, is there a problem?" Mr. Johnson asked.

In a blink, Goldar was gone and Mr. Johnson was again sitting at his desk, looking quite startled. Kimberly then realized the other students were also staring at her. She tried to come up with an explanation, but couldn't think of anything that made a bit of sense. Had she just dreamed the whole thing? she wondered.

The bell rang. Students gathered their belongings and dropped their exams on Mr. Johnson's desk as they exited. Kimberly picked up her books and slowly walked toward the front of the classroom. For a moment she stood in front of Mr. Johnson's desk, looking at her incomplete exam. She sighed, feeling quite disappointed in herself.

Mr. Johnson took Kimberly's exam and disapprovingly looked it over. "Doesn't look like you aced this one like you usually do."

"Not even close," Kimberly admitted shamefully.

Mr. Johnson gave Kimberly a stone-cold glare that made her feel even worse. Then he dropped her exam in the wastepaper basket. "Some of your friends will be in here tomorrow for a makeup exam. Any interest in joining them?"

Kimberly let out a big sigh of relief. "You're a real lifesaver, Mr. Johnson. Thank you so much," she said gratefully. "And if I've never said so before, you really are the best teacher ever."

"I know. Just don't tell anybody. You'll ruin my reputation," Mr. Johnson said. "And nice job at the gymnastics tournament. That was one doozy of a vault."

An hour later, Kimberly was sitting alone in the school cafeteria, glaring at a goopy spoonful of whatever the chef had cooked up that day. She looked at the empty spaces around the table and realized just how much she missed the other Rangers. It had been only two days, but at the moment it felt like forever to her.

"Wake up, Little Miss Hart," Bulk said as he stomped up to Kimberly.

Kimberly's eyes snapped open. She hadn't even realized she'd fallen asleep. "What do you nimrods want?" she asked.

Bulk scoffed in offense. "How about some gratitude after we helped your little friend," he said.

"Yeah, and now you're going to help us," Skull said.

Bulk leaned in close and whispered, "We know you know the Pink Ranger, and she owes us some information," he said.

Kimberly rolled her eyes. "What makes you think I know her?" she asked.

Bulk pointed to his own forehead. "Because you both like pink. Duh."

"And we want to know what she knows about the thing we want to know about," Skull added.

Kimberly sighed. She had forgotten about the deal she made with them. "I will pass along the message if the opportunity comes up. Not that I'm saying it ever will," she said.

"Fair enough, but before we go . . ." Skull hesitated to finish. "What are the chances that me and you could go out on a date?" he asked.

Kimberly snarled in disgust. "Let me think.

How's the day after never work for you?"

Skull grinned. "That's my favorite day of the week. I will see you then," he said.

Bulk and Skull exchanged a high five as they strutted away.

Kimberly let out an irritated sigh. She poked her fork at her lunch and picked up a chunk of something that resembled meat and took a sniff. The stink made her gag a little.

"What's wrong, Pink Ranger—lose your appetite?" Goldar asked from somewhere nearby.

Kimberly looked up and saw Goldar standing across the table. The light in his amulet rapidly flickered with pink energy. Kimberly tried to look away from the amulet, but its power was much too strong.

"Pink Ranger, you cannot fight me. You cannot run from me. I am your master now, and you will do as I say," Goldar said.

"You will never be my master. Now get away from me," Kimberly shouted. She stood up, grabbed the table, and flipped it toward Goldar. Before the table had even hit the floor, he vanished.

As she huffed to catch her breath, Kimberly

noticed all of the other students in the cafeteria were staring at her and whispering to one another. With an embarrassed whimper, she sat back down and wondered if the day could possibly get any worse.

Chapter 23

Minutes after the incident in the cafeteria, Kimberly sat nervously trembling in a chair across the desk from Angel Grove High School's principal, Mr. Kaplan. This was the first time she had ever been in any real trouble, so she didn't know what to say, or if she should say anything at all.

"My, oh my. What an unusual situation we have here," Mr. Kaplan said. He rapidly flipped through Kimberly's school file. "An honor roll GPA, an outstanding attendance record, not a single day spent in detention. Judging by what's in this folder, you are a shining example of the type of student Angel Grove prides itself on," he said.

Just as Kimberly was going to speak, Mr. Kaplan closed the folder and banged a fist down on it. "And yet, here we are in this very upsetting situation. What do you have to say for yourself, Miss Hart?" he asked.

Kimberly grimaced and said, "It won't happen again?"

Mr. Kaplan gave Kimberly a crooked stare. "I see. Well, in that case, you should just head to class," he said.

Kimberly perked up, a bit surprised. "Really?" she asked.

"No! Not really," Mr. Kaplan said. He leaned forward for a closer look at Kimberly. "Are you on giggly pills? Don't lie to me. I can tell."

Kimberly scoffed in offense. "No. Never."

"Darn right you're not," Mr. Kaplan agreed. "Join a street gang?"

Kimberly smirked. "I wouldn't even know how to join a street gang."

"That's right, because Angel Grove is a gang-free institution of learning," Mr. Kaplan said proudly. "So what is going on with Kimberly Ann Hart that would cause her to flip over a table in the school cafeteria?"

Kimberly tried to respond, but Mr. Kaplan pressed a finger to his lips, telling her not to say a word. He spun around in his chair and faced the wall and began tapping a finger on the armrest. His rhythm was in perfect sync with the second hand of a little cuckoo clock sitting on the corner of his desk. After a moment, the beat became so hypnotic that Kimberly could hardly keep her eyes open.

"What is wrong with Kimberly Hart?" Mr. Kaplan said. Then after another moment had passed, he said, "Or should I say, what is wrong with the Pink Ranger?"

Kimberly gasped. "What did you just say?"

The chair spun back around and Goldar was now sitting in it. The light in his amulet flickered so fast that Kimberly couldn't hope to escape its hypnotic power. "That's right, Pink Ranger, your mind belongs to me now," Goldar said.

The next thing Kimberly knew, she was standing in the deepest depths of a dark cavern. She frantically looked all around, trying to figure out where she was, but nothing seemed familiar. She tried to call Alpha 5 on her communicator watch, but there was no signal.

"I see you, Pink Ranger. Can you see me?" Goldar asked, his voice echoing through the rocky cavern.

Kimberly's mind was abuzz with confusion as she stumbled through one rocky tunnel after another, hoping against hope to find a way out. "Enough of this, Goldar. Show yourself," she shouted.

A squad of Putty Patrollers swarmed into the chamber and surrounded Kimberly. She raised her fists, ready for a fight, but they didn't attack. "What are you all waiting for?" Kimberly asked.

Goldar emerged, clutching his sword.

"They're waiting to see if you're going to do as you're told," he said. The pink glow in his amulet caused Kimberly to stumble in confusion. "You must know by now that you can never escape me," he said. "You will help me destroy Zordon and the other Rangers."

"N-no. I would never—" Kimberly stuttered, unable to finish. Between the hypnotic power of the amulet and her state of exhaustion, she was losing her will to resist.

Goldar extended a hand to Kimberly.

"You can put an end to this madness. Just take me to the Command Center, and it will all be over," he said.

Kimberly feverishly shook her head around, trying to break the spell, but it was already taking control of her mind.

Goldar took off the amulet and dangled it inches

from Kimberly's face. Her eyes began to glow bright pink.

"Now take me to the Command Center so we may destroy Zordon once and for all," he said.

Against her own will, Kimberly slowly reached out and took Goldar's hand and said, "I will do as you command, Master Goldar."

Chapter 24

In a glimmering sparkle of light, Alpha 5 teleported into the Command Center. He scurried in a panic over to the main control console. "Aye-yi-yi, this is very bad. Very, very bad," he said.

"Alpha 5, please calm yourself," Zordon said. "What did you learn at the power station?"

"How can I calm myself when an EMP is about to destroy every electronic device in Angel Grove and knock out the Command Center with it?" Alpha 5 asked.

"That is indeed distressing. How long before the EMP is set to go off?" Zordon asked.

Alpha 5 pushed a series of buttons on the console and checked the results. "According to these calculations, the EMP will reach full power in exactly eight hours," he said. Then he looked at the clock on the console and saw just over eight hours remained. "That's minutes before the Rangers are scheduled to return on the space bridge."

"Then we must find a way to stop the EMP. If the Command Center is disabled, we would not be able to calibrate the space bridge. I fear the Rangers would be lost forever," Zordon said gravely.

"Aye-yi-yi, how could this get any worse?" Alpha 5 sobbed.

A pink and gold light flared in the middle of the room and then Pink Ranger and Goldar teleported in.

"Oh no. Emergency. Emergency!" Alpha 5 said, dashing around in a panic.

"Well done, Pink Ranger. You will make an excellent apprentice," Goldar said triumphantly.

The Pink Ranger took off her helmet, revealing her glowing pink eyes. "I am ready to carry out your orders, Master Goldar."

"This can't be," Alpha 5 yelped. "Kimberly, you would never betray us."

"It's not her fault," Zordon said. "She's under one of Rita's spells." He then looked at Goldar. "Why are you here?"

Goldar raised a fist. "I'm here to watch my new apprentice destroy you and the other Rangers."

"I'd like to see you try it," Alpha 5 said. He raced

for a large red button on one of the consoles, trying to activate the intruder alert system.

"Pink Ranger, stop him," Goldar ordered.

Kimberly forced Alpha 5 away from the console.

"Now, Pink Ranger, disable him, permanently," Goldar commanded.

"Kimberly, don't do it," Alpha 5 begged.

The pink light flickered in Kimberly's eyes. "I must do as my master commands." She bashed a fist into the electronic panel on Alpha 5's back, causing sparks to fly and his systems to go offline.

"Zordon, please help meeeeeeee—" Alpha 5 cried, and then slumped over.

"Excellent work, my apprentice," Goldar said. He gave Alpha 5 a shove, knocking him into a corner on the far side of the room. "Now, do away with Zordon once and for all," he said.

"Kimberly, you have the power within yourself to overcome this wicked spell," Zordon said.

Kimberly flicked a series of switches on the control console. She then entered a secret system lockout code. A siren sounded and red lights flashed. Inside the energy chamber, Zordon rapidly faded in and out and then finally vanished.

"At last, Zordon is gone and soon the Power Rangers will be destroyed," Goldar hailed. "And it is all thanks to you, my new apprentice."

"I do as you command, Master Goldar," Kimberly said.

A shadowy sphere formed in the center of the chamber. Streaks of lightning crackled all around it. When the sphere faded away, Rita Repulsa emerged, clutching her staff. "After ten thousand years, the Command Center is finally mine," she shrieked.

Goldar knelt before Rita. "My queen, your plan worked perfectly. There will be nobody to stop us this time."

"Of course my plan worked. I am a mastermind of evil, after all," Rita declared. "And once that EMP goes kaboom, I'll be doing some serious remodeling around here."

"Yes, this will make a perfect base for you to rule over the Earth," Goldar said.

"I believe you are right," Rita said. "Now where is that foolish Finster?"

"I sent him to the power station with a squad of Putty Patrollers to guard the EMP," Goldar said. He led Rita over to the viewing globe. There, they saw Angel

Grove was still in chaos. "With the city nearly drained of power, I knew it would only be a matter of time before the humans would uncover our plan," he said.

"That weakling Finster couldn't guard a block of moldy cheese from a pack of rats. Get to the power station and guard that EMP with your life," Rita commanded.

Chapter 25

At the Angel Grove Power Station, a team of engineers was hard at work trying to determine the cause of the citywide power outage. They had tracked the problem to the electricity generator that was powering up the EMP. Just when an engineer noticed the sinister device, Finster and a squad of Putty Patrollers arrived.

"Putties, show the humans out," Finster said.

The Putty Patrollers swarmed around the engineers and shoved them toward the staircase. The engineers were too terrified to put up a fight. Right as they started heading up, Goldar came stomping down and blocked their way. He held his hand over the amulet so they could see him.

"Get back, you worthless humans," Goldar ordered.

The engineers trembled in fear as they backed down the stairs. They cowered, trapped between Goldar and the Putty Patrollers.

"Goldar, what is the meaning of this?" Finster demanded. "The humans were just about to discover our plan."

"It looks like they already have," Goldar said. "If we let them go, they'll call for help, and then we'll have more trouble to deal with." He glared at the engineers. "I am afraid you'll all be staying here until our plan is complete."

In the corner of the Command Center, Alpha 5 started to twitch. His emergency reboot cycle had activated. He started speaking in gibberish as his systems came online.

"Aye-yi-yi," Alpha 5 said when he saw that Zordon was still offline. He noticed Kimberly standing on the far side of the room, still in a hypnotic trance and eyes glowing bright pink. Not far from her, Rita carelessly rummaged through a storage locker, flinging around fragile pieces of equipment.

"It's all up to me now," Alpha 5 said. "Courage. I must have courage."

Alpha 5 started to sit upright, but stopped when Kimberly looked at him. He feared that she would alert Rita, but she just stared at him without a bit of reaction.

"Think, Alpha 5. There must be a way to get through to Kimberly," he said to himself. He dared to move again, this time sitting all the way up and leaning back against a wall. Kimberly still didn't react.

After a moment of pondering, Alpha 5 decided he would try to communicate with Kimberly with sign language. "I hope I get this right," he said. With nervous hands, he signed the words, "Kimberly, can you understand me?"

She crooked her head to the side a little. The pink energy flickered in her eyes.

"Rita is controlling you with a wicked spell. You must fight it," Alpha 5 signed. Kimberly looked to Rita, then back to Alpha 5, and shook her head as if to say no.

"If you do not fight against Rita, the other Rangers will be lost forever," Alpha 5 continued. "They are your friends, and they need you to help them."

For a brief instant, the pink light in Kimberly's eyes faded out. Alpha 5 knew he was getting through to her, but it was going to take more than that to break the spell.

Then Alpha 5 signed, "Think about your friends—Jason and Trini and Billy and Zack. They would fight to protect you, and I know you would fight to protect them."

Kimberly's head twitched a little. Memories of her friends raced through her mind. She recalled the many good times they'd had together, and the many times they'd fought against Rita.

Alpha 5 signed, "Keep fighting, Kimberly. You're not Rita's servant. You're the Pink Ranger."

Kimberly clutched her head. She was starting to overcome the power of the spell, but it still had a strong grip on her mind. Then, with trembling hands, she responded to Alpha 5 in sign language. "What do I have to do?"

"We need to get Rita out of the Command Center," Alpha 5 replied.

Kimberly looked at Rita. The witch was still busy ransacking the storage lockers. Kimberly then signed to Alpha 5, "I can't fight her like this."

"You don't have to," Alpha 5 replied. He pointed to the intruder alert button. "All you have to do is push the button and the security system will do the rest."

Kimberly nodded in understanding and began to

walk over toward the console. Rita noticed she was on the move.

"Hold it right there, Pink Ranger," said Rita. "I didn't say you could move."

Kimberly stopped cold. The intruder alert button was within reach, but as hard as she tried, she couldn't will herself to push it.

"You can do it, Kimberly," Alpha 5 cried out. "Don't let that wicked old witch stop you now."

"Oh, now I see what's happening here," Rita said. She grabbed her staff and stalked toward Alpha 5. "I should have destroyed this meddlesome tin bucket when I had the chance."

"Please, Kimberly, help me," Alpha 5 pleaded.

Kimberly suddenly found the power within herself to overcome the vile spell. "Rita, I will not let you hurt my friends," she said with gritted teeth, and then slammed her fist down on the intruder alert button.

A siren blared. Red emergency lights flashed. Then an energy force field surrounded Rita.

"Curse you, Pink Ranger. I will have my revenge," Rita vowed. The teleporter activated and banished her from the Command Center.

"You did it, Kimberly," Alpha 5 cheered.

"I just hope I never have to do it again," Kimberly said, rubbing her eyes. She looked at the clock over the console. There was less than one hour left before her friends were due to return. "Now we just have to stop Goldar from setting off that EMP, or Zordon and the others will be lost forever."

Chapter 26

Rita landed with a flop on the observation deck of the Moon Palace. When she stumbled to her feet, she saw Squatt sitting on her golden throne. Baboo was fanning him with a large palm leaf. Putty Patrollers were holding iron bowls overflowing with gruesome edibles.

"What is this treachery?" Rita shouted. "I'm gone for a few hours, and you take over the palace?"

Squatt scrambled off the throne. "We were just messing around, my queen," he said.

"We thought you were busy ruling the Earth from the Command Center," Baboo said.

"Get out of my sight," Rita said, swatting Squatt and Baboo with her staff, chasing them out the door. "Now where is that fool Goldar?"

Goldar teleported into the room and stepped up behind Rita. "What do you need, my queen?" he asked.

Startled, Rita clutched a hand to her chest. "How

did you get here so fast? And why aren't you guarding the EMP?"

"You called for me, so here I am," Goldar said.

"Fools. Every last one of you," Rita grumbled. "Now get down there and start wreaking havoc on Angel Grove."

"What happened at the Command Center?" Goldar asked.

"Just shut up and do as I say," Rita squawked.

Goldar snarled in frustration. "As you command, my queen."

At the Command Center, the clock on the console was counting down from fifty-seven minutes. Kimberly watched Alpha 5 frantically typing away on the control console.

"Aye-yi-yi, are you sure you can't remember the code you entered to lock out Zordon's connection to the Command Center?" Alpha 5 asked.

Kimberly frowned. "I'm trying. I just can't."

Alpha 5 put an arm around Kimberly to comfort her. "This was not your fault. That wicked old Rita did this to you."

"I know, but it doesn't make me feel any better," Kimberly admitted.

"Don't you worry. I'll crack that code if it's the last thing I do. Of course if I don't do that soon, it will be the last thing I do," Alpha 5 said gravely.

Kimberly shook her head, refusing to let that happen. "Then you keep working here, and I'll go to the power station and figure out how to stop that EMP."

"I was hoping you would say that," Alpha 5 said gleefully.

The Command Center alarm sounded.

"Aye-yi-yi! Now what?" Alpha 5 asked. He rushed over to the viewing globe. Goldar was in Downtown Angel Grove, wrecking cars and knocking over power poles. "Kimberly, you must get down there and stop Goldar before he destroys the city."

Kimberly shook her head. "No, I think it's a trick to stop me from going to the power station. If Goldar wants a fight, he can find me there."

"But what about his amulet?" Alpha 5 asked. "You could end up right back under that terrible spell."

"Not this time. I've got a plan," Kimberly said. She held out her Power Morpher. "IT'S MORPHIN TIME!"

...

The Pink Ranger somersaulted into the parking lot of the power station. She sprinted toward a squad of Putty Patrollers near the main entrance. Before they could attack, she pulled out her Power Bow and fired off six shots, taking them out with perfect aim.

With a soaring leap, she got up onto the roof of the power station and took cover behind a heating unit.

Goldar teleported into the parking lot.

The Pink Ranger aimed her bow at Goldar's amulet. Before she fired, the flickering pink light in the amulet caused her to hesitate. She could feel Rita's spell trying to again take control of her mind. Her thoughts became twisted and confused.

She remembered attacking Alpha 5 and how she had betrayed Zordon. In the middle of the madness, she suddenly remembered the secret code she had entered into the Command Center computer that knocked Zordon offline.

"Pink Ranger, come out, come out, wherever you are," Goldar called.

The Pink Ranger wanted to call Alpha 5 to tell him about the code, but she worried that Goldar would hear her. She needed to take out the amulet first.

With a calming breath to clear her mind, she aimed her bow at the amulet. Once she had a clear shot, she fired. Goldar never saw it coming. The arrow pierced the amulet, shattering it into a dozen shards.

"I'll get you for that, Pink Ranger," Goldar bellowed. He took flight and soared toward the rooftop.

The Pink Ranger called Alpha 5 on the communicator in her helmet. "Alpha, I know the code to get Zordon back online."

"Then I'm going to help you forget it," Goldar said as he came in for a landing near the Pink Ranger. He then pummeled her with a powerful uppercut, sending her flying backward into a concrete wall.

"Alpha 5 to Kimberly," he called on the communicator. "If you can hear me, please respond."

Chapter 27

On the power station rooftop, Goldar nudged the Pink Ranger with his metal boot, but she didn't react. Her plan to lure Goldar closer by pretending to be unconscious was working perfectly.

"You disappoint me, Pink Ranger," he said. "Without the other Rangers, you're nothing but a weak little girl," Goldar mocked.

"Think again," the Pink Ranger said. She kicked Goldar's legs out from under him and then sprang to her feet.

Just as Goldar struggled back to his feet, the Pink Ranger unleashed a mighty melee of punches and spinning jump kicks, hitting Goldar again and again. Goldar stumbled backward, dizzied and half knocked out.

The Pink Ranger pulled out her Power Bow and aimed an arrow at Goldar. "Now tell me how to shut down the EMP."

"Figure it out yourself," Goldar said. He lurched to the side and knocked the bow from her hand. Before he could attack again, the Pink Ranger spun around and pummeled him with a mighty side kick. Goldar went soaring backward off the building and across the parking lot. He crashed into a truck, smashing it into a pile of twisted steel.

"Alpha 5, transmitting the code now. Get Zordon back online ASAP," Kimberly said into her helmet's communicator.

"Will do," Alpha 5 said gleefully. "What about the EMP?"

"Still working on it," the Pink Ranger replied.

At the Moon Palace, Rita watched the battle through her telescope. Goldar was clawing his way out of the wrecked remains of the truck. "If that foolish Pink Ranger believes she can defeat my best warrior, she's got another thing coming. Magic wand, make my Goldar grow!"

Rita flung her staff toward the Earth. It sailed downward through the atmosphere and all the way to the power station. The staff pierced into the asphalt near Goldar. Lightning bolts of mystical energy shot out, causing Goldar to grow and grow until he towered over fifty feet in height.

Alpha 5 called the Pink Ranger. "You have to teleport out of there. You can't fight him on your own," he yelped.

"How long before the other Rangers return?" the Pink Ranger asked.

"Seven minutes. But if the EMP goes off first, they'll be lost forever," Alpha 5 replied.

"Then I'm going to need help in a big way," Kimberly said.

"I know. I know. I'm working to get Zordon back online right now," Alpha 5 said.

At the Command Center, Alpha 5 typed the security code Kimberly had transmitted into the main computer. "Aye-yi-yi, this better work, or we're doomed."

Inside the energy chamber, Zordon rapidly appeared and then disappeared again. When he spoke, his voice sounded glitchy. "Alpha 5—can you—hear-hear—me?"

"Hold on, Zordon, I just need to make a few adjustments," Alpha 5 said. He flicked a series of switches on the console. "That should do it."

Zordon's form stabilized in the energy chamber. "Good work, Alpha 5. I thank you," he said.

"No time for thanks. Kimberly is in serious trouble," Alpha 5 said.

The Pink Ranger hid out of sight, helplessly watching Goldar rampage a nearby building.

"Pink Ranger, do you read me?" Zordon asked over her communicator.

"Zordon, it's so good to hear your voice," she replied. "I need my Zord now."

"Then you need only to call on it," Zordon replied.

Kimberly raised her arm to the sky. "Pterodactyl Dinozord Power!" she shouted.

From the mouth of a distant volcano, the robotic Pterodactyl Zord rocketed into the sky. It flew at supersonic speed and reached the power station in mere moments. The Pink Ranger leaped into the sky and landed in the pilot's seat. "Now, time to send Goldar back to where he came from," she said.

The Pink Ranger piloted the Pterodactyl Zord toward Goldar. He tried to swat the Zord from the sky, but the Pink Ranger made a hard turn to evade the strike. She targeted Goldar and fired a full burst of shots from the Zord's energy cannons.

Goldar stumbled off balance, but quickly recovered. "You'll have to do better than that if you want to stop me, Pink Ranger," he jeered.

Chapter 28

Inside the power station, a squad of Putty Patrollers guarded the captive engineers.

Finster checked the power gauge on the EMP. The needle was a hair below the FULL line. "It will only be minutes now, which means it's time for me to get out of here," he said.

The Putty Patrollers followed Finster as he headed toward the stairs. "Get back, you brainless oafs," he said. "You must stay here to make sure nothing disrupts the detonation."

The Putty Patrollers exchanged nervous stares.

High above the power station, the Pink Ranger maneuvered the Pterodactyl Zord around for another attack run against Goldar. She knew there was no time left to spare. If there was a chance to stop the EMP from going off, it had to happen now.

Twenty yards behind Goldar, the Pink Ranger spotted a pair of electrical towers with thick power lines strung in between. She throttled the engines to maximum speed and set her targeting sights at Goldar's feet.

The Pterodactyl Zord's cannons fired a barrage of energy bolts. Goldar roared and retreated back, stepping closer to the power lines. The Pink Ranger then fired a volley of missiles. The ground exploded beneath Goldar's feet.

Goldar roared furiously and stumbled into the power lines. Bolts of electricity zapped through his armor. He plummeted into the ground with a thunderous rumble. One of his hulking arms crashed down atop the power station, destroying most of the building.

The Pink Ranger ejected from the Pterodactyl Zord and dropped down to the ground near the station entrance. The engineers were fleeing from the building. Putty Patrollers raced out and scattered in a panic. Goldar was still tangled in the power lines and unable to stand, though the Pink Ranger suspected he would soon break free.

The Pink Ranger climbed over mounds of busted

concrete and twisted steel. She found the staircase leading to the lower levels of the station. Smoke and ash soiled the air, making it difficult for her to see where she was going.

When she reached the lowest level of the station, it took her nearly a minute to locate the EMP. The needle on the power gauge was twitching at the FULL line, and a timer was counting down from three minutes.

"Alpha 5, I have the EMP," she said into her communicator. "It's fully charged and set to go off in three minutes."

"Aye-yi-yi," Alpha 5 replied. "It will be almost four minutes until the space bridge opens. If you don't find a way to stop the EMP from going off, the other Rangers will be lost forever."

Zordon then said, "Kimberly, you must use the Pterodactyl Zord to get the EMP as far away from the city as possible."

The Pink Ranger hurried out of the power station, lugging the bulky EMP in her arms.

"But if the EMP goes off while she's in flight, her Zord would be disabled," Alpha 5 yelped. "That would mean—"

The Pink Ranger interrupted, "It would mean my Zord would lose control and maybe even crash. But it's the only chance we have, so I have to take it." She carefully put the EMP on the ground and checked the timer: It was now down to two minutes.

With a skyward leap, the Pink Ranger again landed in the pilot's seat of the Pterodactyl Zord. She slowed the thrusters and maneuvered around so she could scoop up the EMP in the Zord's mighty jaw.

Goldar finally untangled himself from the power lines. He scrambled to his feet and saw what was happening. With a furious roar, he swung his arm, trying to thwack the Pterodactyl Zord from the sky. The Pink Ranger steered into a tight turn, just dodging his gigantic hand.

The Pink Ranger angled her Zord skyward and cranked the thrusters up to maximum power. The force of the takeoff slammed her back into her seat. "Alpha 5, what's the minimum altitude to make sure this thing doesn't knock out the Command Center?" she asked.

"At least fifty miles, but the higher the better," Alpha 5 replied.

Zordon added, "Pink Ranger, you must power

down the Pterodactyl Zord's computer right before the EMP detonates. It's the only chance to protect the Zord's electronics from being destroyed in the blast. You will then need two minutes to restart the systems."

"Understood," the Pink Ranger replied, hoping against hope that she could keep her Zord in the air long enough not to crash. When the computer indicated that she'd reached the needed altitude, she took a deep breath and said, "Pink Ranger, going offline. Wish me luck."

The Pink Ranger powered off the main computer. The Pterodactyl Zord's thrusters shut down. The EMP detonated. Thousands of searing lightning bolts shot in every direction. The Zord's dense armor shielded the Pink Ranger from the brunt of the blast, but it wasn't enough to save her from being zapped out of her senses.

Chapter 29

"Calling the Pink Ranger. Come in, Pink Ranger," Alpha 5 desperately said into the communicator. On the Command Center viewing globe, he watched the Pterodactyl Zord plummeting through the clouds. "Oh, why won't she respond?"

Zordon said, "Her Zord's systems haven't restarted, and her communicator might have been damaged by the EMP. There is nothing we can do but wait and hope. In the meantime, you must enter the coordinates to align the space bridge, or the other Rangers will be lost."

"Aye-yi-yi, I nearly forgot," Alpha 5 said. He scampered over to the main control console and typed in the computations. The clock counted down to zero. "Engaging space bridge now," he said.

An energy spear opened up on the transport platform. Jason, Zack, Billy, and Trini stepped through. Filth and muck covered them from head to toe, and they were ambling in exhaustion.

"Mission accomplished, Zordon," Jason said. "I think we're all going to need to sleep for about a month, though."

Zordon proudly looked at the Rangers. "I'm pleased to learn of your success, but we have an urgent situation."

The Pterodactyl Zord's computer finished its automatic reboot cycle. Lights on the control panel lit up. A warning alarm sounded. The Pink Ranger finally began to come to her senses. She cried out in distress when she saw her Zord was plummeting downward on a collision course to the power station. She desperately pulled back on the control stick. Nothing happened.

"Alpha, can you hear me? Please come in," she said on the communicator.

"Alpha 5, receiving your signal. It's good to hear your voice, Kimberly," he excitedly replied.

"You won't be hearing me for long unless I get the thrusters started," the Pink Ranger said.

"Just push the starter button by your left knee and

be ready to feel a major kick," Alpha 5 warned.

The Pink Ranger took a deep breath and pushed the button. The engines ignited with a thunderous roar. The force slammed her back into her seat. She pulled back on the control stick. The Zord began to gradually arc out of the dive.

"Alpha, I'm not pulling up fast enough," she yelped.

"Don't give up," Alpha 5 urged. "The other Rangers are here, and we all know you can do it."

The Pink Ranger gritted her teeth and pulled back on the control stick with all of her might. Mere feet before hitting the ground, the Zord finally leveled out. Its bottom scraped across a patch of trees as it started to soar upward.

The Pink Ranger howled in victory. "I am never doing that again." She smiled when she heard Alpha 5 and the other Rangers cheering on the communicator.

"Good work, Pink Ranger. We knew you could do it," Zordon said.

The Pink Ranger spotted Goldar stalking through Downtown Angel Grove. "We can celebrate later. Tell the other Rangers to meet me downtown and bring backup. It's time to put an end to this nightmare."

...

At the Command Center, Jason took out his Power Morpher. "You heard her, team. IT'S MORPHIN TIME!"

Zack shouted, "Mastodon," and he morphed into the Black Ranger.

Billy shouted, "Triceratops," and he morphed into the Blue Ranger.

Trini shouted, "Sabertooth Tiger," and she morphed into the Yellow Ranger.

Jason shouted, "Tyrannosaurus," and he morphed into the Red Ranger.

The four Power Rangers arrived in Downtown Angel Grove. Goldar was stomping down Main Street, crushing cars and knocking over street lamps. The Pterodactyl Zord swooped overhead, firing a volley of energy bolts at Goldar.

The Red Ranger spoke into his communicator. "This is your fight to lead, Kimberly."

The Pink Ranger replied, "We need Dinozord power, now."

From distant corners of the Earth, the four robotic

Zords arose from their hidden lairs. Moments later, they arrived in Angel Grove, roaring furiously and ready for battle.

The four Rangers leaped high into the air and landed in the cockpits of their Zords. The Red Ranger commanded the Tyrannosaurus Dinozord. The Blue Ranger commanded the Triceratops Dinozord. The Yellow Ranger commanded the Sabertooth Tiger Dinozord. The Black Ranger commanded the Mastodon Dinozord.

"Now it's time for some Megazord action," the Pink Ranger hollered.

The five Dinozords began combining into a single robotic machine. The Sabertooth Tiger and Triceratops Zords became the legs. The Mastodon transformed into a pair of hulking arms. The Tyrannosaurus became the torso that linked all the parts together. The Pterodactyl took the form of an armored chest plate and merged with the mighty machine. Once complete, the Megazord towered over 150 feet in height and weighed one hundred tons.

All five Rangers now sat in a single command cockpit. "Time to put an end to that metal menace

Goldar once and for all," the Pink Ranger said.

Goldar dashed toward the Megazord and punched it several times in the chest. "You puny Rangers can't defeat me."

"Let's show him what we can do, team," the Pink Ranger shouted. The Megazord punched Goldar repeatedly, then leaped high and pummeled him with a double front kick in the chest.

"Fire concussion rockets," the Pink Ranger said. A volley of rockets fired from the shoulders of the Megazord. Each hit Goldar with thunderously explosive blasts. He crashed down with an earth-rumbling thud.

"It's over, Goldar. This is your last chance to surrender," the Pink Ranger shouted.

Goldar got to his feet. "I'll never surrender to you," he bellowed. Then he extended an arm, and a sword appeared in his hand.

The Red Ranger raised his fist skyward. "I call on the Power Sword." A massive, gleaming sword appeared in the hand of the Megazord. "Now let's finish this," he said.

The Megazord and Goldar exchanged a thunderous series of sword strikes. Explosive sparks scattered as the titans viciously hacked and slashed at one another. Finally, the Megazord knocked Goldar's sword from his hand, and then continued hacking and slashing into his armor.

As Goldar stumbled off balance, the Megazord walloped him with a kick to the torso. Goldar crashed to the ground, gasping and unable to continue the fight.

"You're finished, Goldar," the Pink Ranger said. The Megazord swung the Power Sword to deal the final blow.

"Not today, Pink Ranger, but I'll be back," Goldar vowed. He teleported away, just before the Power Sword sliced him in two.

"And the Power Rangers will be ready when you are," the Pink Ranger said with a fist raised in victory. "Let's go home, team. I could really use a nap right about now."

The other Rangers nodded in wholehearted agreement.

Chapter 30

Later that evening at the Juice Bar, Jason, Zack, Billy, and Trini entered, carrying Kimberly on their shoulders.

Kimberly held up her first-place trophy from the *Toughest Warrior* contest. Sarah, Jack, and many of the students from the Center for the Hearing Impaired followed along.

"Who's the Toughest Warrior?" Jason asked using sign language.

"Kimberly is the Toughest Warrior," everyone signed together.

They carried Kimberly to a table and sat her in a chair. She did her best to hold back a yawn, but the thrill of victory was no match for how tired she felt.

Ernie approached with a tray stacked with enough drinks for everyone. "To honor your victory celebration, I offer this delightful assortment of fruity drinks, all on the house."

"You're the best, Ernie. Thank you," Kimberly said with a smile, and then picked up a drink.

Ernie started to sign. "And I thank you for teaching me to speak in sign language."

Kimberly and the others giggled.

"Did I do it wrong again?" Ernie asked timidly.

"It was a good try, Ernie," Kimberly said.

Ernie chuckled uneasily and hurried away.

Jack stood up and signed, "I would like to thank our wonderful friend Kimberly Hart. Her victory has assured the Center will remain open."

Everyone clapped and cheered.

Kimberly handed Jack an envelope. "And here is the check—signed, sealed, and delivered."

"That's a lot of money. Are you sure you want to donate all of it?" Sarah asked.

"Think of all the shopping you could do," Jack signed.

"Saving the Center is more important than shopping," Kimberly replied, then smiled slightly. "Then again, there is this really cool leather jacket I've been eyeing."

"Consider it yours if you want it," Jack replied.

"Nah, I need to leave my mom something to get me for Christmas," she replied.

"Thank you for everything. You're the best friend I've ever had," Sarah signed, and then hugged Kimberly.

"Kimberly Hart, you can't get away from me so easily," a bellowing voice shouted from nearby.

"Not again," Kimberly said with a fright, thinking Goldar had returned. She let out a long sigh of relief when she saw it was only Bulk and Skull stomping her way.

Bulk held up a finger. "First thing, I checked and there is no such thing as the day after never. If you didn't want to go out with me, you could have just said so," he said.

"Okay, I don't want to go out with you," Kimberly said.

"Fair enough." Bulk sulked. He then held up two fingers. "Second thing, you owe us some information."

Jason stepped up and glared at Bulk. "Kimberly, you okay?" he asked.

"Yeah, I've got this." Kimberly smirked a little. She then leaned in close to Bulk and whispered,

"I got an answer from the one you asked me to ask about that thing you wanted to know about."

"And what did she say?" Bulk asked excitedly.

Kimberly used sign language to say, "The tale of Bobo the Pirate King is an urban legend and there is no treasure."

"Hey, you know we don't speak handfu. I mean, uh, sign language," Bulk said.

"Yeah, tell us what all that hand stuff means," Skull said.

"Sorry," Kimberly sneered. "It's not my fault you two can't understand her message, but that's the way she delivered it. Now get lost."

Jason gave Bulk and Skull a tough stare down. They knew better than to mess with him and took off in a bitter huff.

Jason sat down by Kimberly. "Zordon said you handled things like a champ while we were away. Sounds like you're ready for the Pan Global Games."

"Maybe so." Kimberly grinned at the thought of this. "For now, I think I'm going to take a nap."

"You mean right here and now?" Jason asked.

"Yep. Right here. Right now. I think I've earned it,"

she said, and leaned back in her chair. Then finally, after three long days of nonstop action, Kimberly Ann Hart's eyes flicked shut and she drifted off into a peaceful slumber.

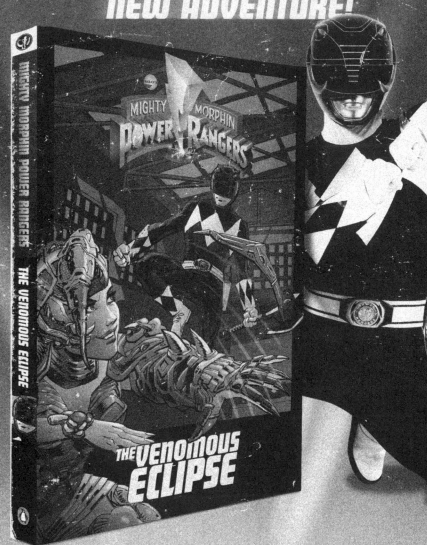